# ETHERIC RECRUIT

# ETHERIC RECRUIT

ETHERIC ADVENTURES: ANNE AND JINX BOOK ONE

SR RUSSELL

MICHAEL ANDERLE

DISRUPTIVE IMAGINATION

LMBPN Publishing
PMB 196, 2540 South Maryland Pkwy
Las Vegas, NV 89109

First US edition, September 2017
Version 1.01, December 2017

# CHAPTER ONE

*Dead.*

*I'm so freakin' dead*, thought the girl, as she tried desperately to hold back her tears.

Crying at school would just make matters worse. She didn't need her classmates to be on her case for being a cry baby. As it was, the D she had just received on her chemistry test would be enough for her parents to ground her for two weeks...again.

Anne had constantly been in trouble with her parents for the last couple of years now. They claimed she was acting out because they had been required to leave their old life behind when some very bad people threatened her and her mom to make her dad do what they wanted.

Her parents seemed to have forgotten that Anne was the one who had sent a letter to Bethany Anne to ask for help.

The truth of the matter was, Anne just felt so tired nowadays that it was hard for her to stay awake, let alone focus, in class. And she hurt so much her aches had aches. *Not normal*, she thought, *for a sixteen-year-old girl*.

Her parents insisted that she was only suffering growing pains, which in their minds were no excuse for bad grades. They had been very clear in stating they expected her to excel.

Failing the entrance examination for the Etheric Academy had resulted in her being grounded for a week.

*To heck with it*, thought Anne Jayden. Knowing she would be subject to yet another lecture and probably grounded *again*, Anne decided to take a detour on her way home.

She, and probably ninety-nine-point-nine percent of the people on the *Meredith Reynolds*, knew that Bellatrix and Ashur had had a litter of puppies. She hadn't been able to see any of them yet.

Heck, she thought to herself, she hadn't even seen Ashur in person for the last couple of years. As things had gotten worse on Earth and the Etheric Empire headed into Yollin space, her parents Mason and Sheila Jayden had forbidden her to go near the Queen's quarters. This meant that not only could she not talk to Bethany Anne, but she didn't get to play with Ashur anymore either.

Anne decided to go to Yelena's quarters, hoping she could see Bellatrix and some of the puppies for a little while. She'd get some video of them on her tablet so she could watch it as she served the prison sentence her parents would impose as soon as she returned home.

Anne exited the tram and walked to the intersection nearest Yelena's quarters. Leaning against the wall, she crossed her fingers and hoped that Yelena or one of the dogs would show up soon, since she wasn't quite forward enough to knock on the door. Thirty minutes later she sighed in defeat and walked back to the tram station to head home and face the music.

Anne couldn't help sigh as the door hadn't opened completely before ...

"Where have you been young lady?"

———

Jinx looked at the chew toy and sighed as she laid her head on her paws. She, her siblings and parents were the most advanced, intelligent canines known to exist, thanks to Kurtherian nanotech.

It was somewhat ironic that they still had an urge to chew.

Their dad's human had threatened to turn them into throw rugs if anyone chewed on her shoes. They had all decided that despite the wonderful way they smelled, shoes were off limits.

It was a good thing humans were so accommodating towards their four-footed companions. People had created a myriad of items that satisfied the desire to chew.

It wasn't the chew toy that had caused the sigh, however. Jinx was feeling a restlessness, something close to failure. It sat in her mind like an itch on the top of her back that she couldn't scratch.

Once she and her siblings had reached an age where they could learn to understand the noises the humans made, their dad had told them the story of how he had met his human, Bethany Anne.

Their mom's human had mentioned how the people of Earth bought and sold animals without regard for the animal's feelings or desires. All five of the puppies decided that they didn't think that sort of thing was in their best interest. They informed Yelena they would choose their own companion person.

After all, it was family tradition. Ashur had chosen, way back when, to help Bethany Anne fight the-stinky-like-death-but-not-dead creatures, and to share her life afterwards.

Jinx sighed again, wondering if something was wrong with her. Three of her siblings had already found their companions. Matrix and Snow had even chosen aliens to pair up with.

Jinx didn't think she would be happy pairing with an alien. She secretly didn't know how Snow put up with the smell of Kael-ven, because all the beings called Yollins had a slightly bitter odor to Jinx' nose.

She was just contemplating heading to bed for a nap when she heard the door to their den open.

She snorted at the thought. It wasn't a den, but she had learned that others of the canine genus on Earth lived in dens, so that's how she thought of Yelena's apartment.

A sharp bark followed by a higher pitched bark announced the arrival of her dad, coming to visit her mom.

---

"Here." Anne forwarded her chemistry test results to her mother's tablet. "I knew I was going to get yelled at again, so do you blame me for not being in a hurry to get home?"

Anne flinched and took a step backwards at the look of anger that crossed her mother's face.

*"Go. To. Your. Room. Now!"* Her mother spat the words one at a time.

Anne spun silently on her toes and headed for her room, her mother's voice following her down the short hallway.

"With that attitude, you can go without supper too! It'll give you time to think about your behavior."

Anne sighed to herself, being very careful not to let anything show in her posture as she turned to enter her bedroom.

Just yesterday she hadn't felt well enough to want to eat supper, yet her mother had forced her to sit and eat at the family table.

Her mother, as usual, hadn't noticed her being sick an hour later when the unwanted meal refused to remain in her stomach. Not wanting to risk getting into more trouble, she followed the rules and left her bedroom door open behind her as she headed for her desk.

She couldn't risk lying on her bed right now, because if she happened to fall asleep when she was supposed to be studying, it was just going to make matters that much worse.

Anne settled into the chair and pulled out her tablet in an attempt to complete the history assignment that was due in two days. She was doing her best to get through it, making sure to look focused so that when her mother came by to check on her she wouldn't be subjected to further disciplinary actions.

Jinx got up and made her way into the main room to find Ashur and Bellatrix rubbing noses. "Oh, gross. What is it humans say? Get a room, you two!"

"Lighten up, Jinx." Yelena laughed as she entered the room from the kitchen. "If we're comparing dogs to humans, that's the equivalent of a hello kiss, not some sort of make-out session."

Ashur took the time to rub his cheek against Bellatrix, then turned to his daughter. "You seem to be in a bad mood today. What is wrong?"

Jinx sat and looked at Yelena, Bellatrix, and Ashur. "Humans call it 'feeling sorry for yourself'. Everyone except Dio and me has found their partners. Heck, Matrix and Snow have partnered with aliens. One of them is a being who lives in your person's head," Jinx replied, looking at Ashur.

"I wonder if something is wrong with me, that I can't find someone I feel right about." Jinx' head drooped a little as she expressed one of her fears.

"Well, you won't find someone if you sit in here all day," Ashur told her with a faint growl. "Let's go for a walk and we can talk over ideas to help you meet more people."

"Are you guys good, or do you need me for anything?" Yelena asked the assembled canines.

After a moment, the dogs told her that they would be fine without Yelena's presence.

Yelena smiled and announced she was going to go see what kind of trouble Bobcat was getting into.

All the canines had become accustomed to certain

human behaviors. Take human smiles, for instance. They had needed to learn that the showing of teeth was not a sign of aggression.

They just shook their heads when Yelena disappeared into her bedroom, muttering about needing to change into something nicer.

Bellatrix, Ashur, and Jinx left the apartment. As they headed for the tram station, Jinx was distracted by an enticing smell on the wall at the first intersection. Ashur and Bellatrix had turned the corner and were several paces away before they realized Jinx was no longer with them.

"What did you find?" Ashur asked Jinx as the two adults returned to their offspring.

"The smell of this person is really different. I wonder who it is?" Jinx answered, still sniffing the wall.

Ashur inhaled the scent that had intrigued Jinx, and realized with a shock that he was familiar with it.

It belonged to the young girl he and his human had rescued. He remembered chasing a ball for her after they moved her and her family to safety on the other ship. "That smells like Anne," Ashur informed Jinx. "We rescued her from some bad people once."

"Do you know where to find her?" Jinx asked, almost quivering with excitement.

"No," Ashur watched his daughter's tail droop at his answer, "but I see Yelena coming and we can get her to ask Bethany Anne for you."

Now wearing a pair of black slacks that weren't decorated with dog hair and a robin's-egg blue blouse, Yelena was surprised to see the three dogs stopped just down the hallway from her apartment.

"Don't you guys get any hair on my clean pants!" She told them as she approached the corner. Desiring her assistance, all three dogs sat along the wall and looked at her expectantly. "What?" Yelena asked, wondering about the strange behavior.

"Would you please ask Bethany Anne where the girl we rescued—Anne—now lives?" Ashur requested.

"Okay …" Yelena replied, somewhat confused. "Meredith, would you please see if her Most Exalted Empress Bethany Anne has a moment to talk with me?"

# CHAPTER TWO

Bethany Anne, Queen Bitch and Empress of the Etheric Empire, was sitting with her feet up looking at some of the new designs ADAM was showing her. They were the result of a collaboration between him and the Ex-President's oldest daughter to produce some new purses.

"Why purses?" Bethany Anne asked.

>>**You have such a love of shoes that we wanted to start with something that would have less negative impact if you didn't like the design. But it also needed to be something that would allow us to work with the new materials available here on Yoll. If we can design and manufacture purses, then the next step will be footwear.**<<

"Makes sense," Bethany Anne muttered to ADAM, then closed her eyes when Meredith's voice came over the room's speakers.

"Bethany Anne, Yelena has asked me to ask the Most Exalted Empress if she remembers rescuing a girl named Anne?"

"Put me through to Yelena please, Meredith." Bethany Anne sat straight in her chair, waiting for the connection.

"You are connected with Yelena," Meredith confirmed seconds later.

"Yelena, I wonder how your attitude might change if you had one of my exalted boots up your butt," Bethany Anne asked her friend. "Besides yanking my chain, what did you want?"

"Ashur is with me, and he is asking if you know where the girl you rescued, Anne is her name, lives."

*ADAM, what was Anne's last name, and do you have a residence location for her?*

>>**Anne Jayden. You rescued them in Las Vegas. The Jaydens live in Residential Section 5A, Apartment 17.**<<

*Thank you.*

"Yelena, tell Furball that the family he's looking for is the Jaydens, and they live in 5A-17," Bethany Anne relayed.

"Thanks, Bethany Anne, will do," replied Yelena.

---

"Where is that?" asked Jinx, since all the dogs had heard Bethany Anne's reply to Yelena.

"I'm not positive," Yelena said to an expectant Jinx. "Meredith, how would we get to 5A-17?"

"Take the tram inward for two stops. Exit at the second stop, and I'll have a hover cart there to guide you to the apartment," Meredith answered.

"Thanks, Yelena. Have fun with Bobcat," Jinx told the woman as she turned toward the tram stop.

Two tram stops later, Jinx jumped on the hover cart

that Meredith had waiting for them. It was only a short walk, or ride in Jinx' case, before the three dogs were standing in front of a door with the number 17 marked on it.

Ashur was tall enough that he could nose the doorbell while keeping all four feet on the ground.

---

Sheila was in the kitchen, getting supper started for her husband and herself when the apartment's EI announced that there were guests at the front door. Muttering, "Who could that be?" She washed her hands and walked to the apartment entrance.

Sheila opened the door, wondering if possibly one of her daughter's friends had come over. "Anne is grounded and not allowed visi ..." Sheila sputtered to a stop as the door opened to reveal three dogs.

"We would like to see Anne for a moment, please," Ashur politely asked the woman who came to the door. From her looks and scent, Ashur was certain he was talking to Anne's mother.

Since the seven dogs of the Etheric Empire were capable of speech, and with the move to Yollin space, every citizen of Bethany Anne's Empire was entitled to a free implant that would allow them to be able to communicate with any non-humans.

If Sheila Jayden had taken advantage of this, she would have heard Ashur ask politely to see her daughter. Instead, what she heard was a series of barks and growls. Shocked and a little afraid, Sheila took a half-step back from the large white dog that was standing at the door barking at her.

---

Anne didn't have an implant either, since her mother didn't understand or acknowledge the need for such a device. Anne had just about reached the end of the required reading when a noise caught her attention. Was that...barking?

Forgetting that she was supposed to be restricted to her room, Anne dashed to the front door and slid to a stop just behind her mother. "Ashur!" Anne shouted, seeing the big white dog at the door. "Oh, puppy!" she said a second later as a smaller German Shepherd that was frantically wagging its tail caught her attention.

Jinx had been content to let her sire take the lead while meeting with these new humans. She watched as the adult human stepped backward while putting her hands to her face, but suddenly Jinx' attention shifted to a smaller human who had slid to a stop behind the bigger one.

Jinx worked her nose to sort out all the odors. *Yes!* The human girl had the interesting smell that had caught her attention in the corridor near her home. Something inside Jinx seemed to shift, and she felt an overwhelming desire to be with the girl. Jinx was so focused on Anne as she started walking into the dwelling that she completely missed the mother's reaction.

Sheila Jayden wasn't a happy camper. In fact, she hadn't been a happy camper for a long time.

She understood that her husband and family had to be

part of the Etheric Empire for security reasons. After all, being held hostage to make your husband divulge confidential information from his work hadn't been much fun, and she had no desire for a repeat.

However, understanding something and being happy about it were two completely different things. Sheila had never been happy about leaving Las Vegas.

The stupid chunk of rock she now lived in didn't have a country club, didn't have any nightlife, and didn't have cruises to Alaska and Hawaii.

When she saw one of those animals, the kind that dug holes in the yard and left hair all over the place, try to get into her apartment, she screamed. "No, you don't!" and lashed out with her foot, kicking Jinx in the ribs and knocking her backward.

Anne was standing behind her mother, almost in a daze. She knew Ashur, and he was at her door, but she couldn't take her eyes off the puppy. She knelt down with her arms wide when the puppy started toward her, and could almost feel the pain in her side when her mother kicked it in the ribs.

"No!" Anne cried as she darted past her mother and squeezed between the now-growling Ashur and Bellatrix to get to the pup, who was just getting back to her feet.

Anne flopped down beside the pup and reached out slowly. "Are you okay?" She asked the pup, slowly running her hand down its side and carefully watching for any sign of pain.

SR RUSSELL & MICHAEL ANDERLE

"Bethany Anne, it appears we have a problem. Video feed on your screen now." Meredith's voice interrupted Bethany Anne as she sat scanning reports of the continued unrest on the planet Yoll.

"Is this live?" Bethany Anne asked as she saw Ashur and Bellatrix in a doorway. It looked like they were threatening a woman who was inside, and there was a young lady outside the door who was on her knees running her hand over one of the puppies.

"Yes, apparently there is some issue between the dogs and Sheila Jayden. I noticed it from the video camera on the hover cart I sent to guide Ashur and his family to the Jayden residence. I don't have audio at this time so I don't know the details of what is occurring, but the video shows that the woman kicked the puppy for some reason."

Bethany Anne thought Meredith almost sounded offended. "Can you pan out so I can see more of the area, please? I need a bigger picture of the area to port there."

"Switching cameras," Meredith informed her, and Bethany Anne now had a view from one of the security cams that lined some of the public hallways. It didn't give her the view into the apartment the way the camera on the hover cart did, but it provided a clear view of several feet of the hall outside the apartment door.

"That's great, thanks." Bethany Anne replied. She laid down her tablet and rose from her seat, then took one step and disappeared.

---

Bethany Anne arrived in time to stop Ashur or Bellatrix

from taking a piece out of Anne's mother. She grabbed the two growling dogs by their scruffs, one in each hand, and dragged them both from the apartment.

She gave them both a shake as she released them. "Enough, you two! What's going on here?" While no fangs were showing, the tinge of red in her eyes would have alerted everyone who knew her to the fact that Bethany Anne wasn't very happy right now.

"That woman kicked our daughter!" Ashur told his alpha. He'd seen the red eyes often enough that he wasn't overly concerned.

Feeling braver now that someone had the dogs under control, and still not understanding that the dogs were actually talking, Sheila darted out, planning to grab Anne and drag her back into the apartment.

Jinx, seeing the older woman heading for her person, jumped between Anne and her mother. "If you touch my person, I'll bite you!" Jinx warned the woman.

Sheila only heard more barks and growls. Not yet realizing the identity of the woman who had shown up and taken care of the two big dogs, she snapped, "Get that filthy mutt away from my daughter!"

"Jinx is not filthy, nor is she a mutt, and I believe she has chosen your daughter as her person, so you'd best heed her warning. It was given clearly enough," Bethany Anne informed Sheila.

"Growling at a person isn't a warning, it's a threat!" Sheila cried. "Those animals shouldn't be able to threaten people! And what's this 'she's chosen her' nonsense?"

Bethany Anne was speechless for a moment, trying to understand what Sheila was saying.

>>A check of their health records indicates that the Jaydens do not have the latest implant.<<

*How did we miss them?*

>>We didn't. The wife has repeatedly refused the implant for herself and her daughter. In fact, if the husband didn't require one for work, I suspect he would not have one either.<<

*She just hears barks and growls?*

>>Correct.<<

*Thanks, ADAM.*

"Mother, she said if you touch me she'll bite you, and you should remember or at least recognize our Empress, Bethany Anne." Anne waved a hand at Bethany Anne as she sat beside Jinx. "Ashur! Hiya, buddy. Who's this lovely lady?" Anne asked, her gaze focused on Bellatrix.

"That's my mom, Bellatrix, and my name is Jinx and I choose you as my person," Jinx finished with a joyous yip.

"Hello, Bellatrix." Anne held out a hand for the big black dog to sniff.

"If I'm your person, does that mean you're my dog?" Anne asked Jinx.

"Yes, yes," Jinx was wagging her tail so hard she repeatedly hit Anne in the back with it. "I'm Jinx. You, me, together!" Jinx told her.

"Wait a minute," Bethany Anne interrupted, holding up one hand. "You understand what Jinx is saying?" She recalled what ADAM had just told her about implants.

Anne nodded as Ashur interjected, "She's always been able to understand me, even before that last treatment in the Pod thingy."

"Shit, you're right. I had forgotten about that," Bethany Anne muttered.

"I don't know what kind of crazy stunt this is, but Anne is grounded, and she is *not* allowed to have a pet! I don't care if you are a queen or empress, I won't have one of those shedding fuzzballs in my house," Sheila virtually spat, anger replacing the fear she had felt just moments ago when faced with growling dogs.

Bethany Anne had heard just about enough. "Cluck like a chicken," she ordered, looking directly into Sheila Jayden's eyes.

Sheila thought she saw a flash of red in Bethany Anne's eyes. *What the hell are you talking about?* came out as a rather angry-sounding "cluck cluck cluck," as did *What is going on?* Regardless of what Sheila thought, when she tried to say the words out loud the only sound she could produce was *cluck*.

"Enough." Bethany Anne waved a hand almost negligently. "You can stop clucking now. But you might want to think about who you are talking to before you start making claims you can't back up."

Although she didn't like doing it, Bethany Anne did a quick scan of Sheila's thoughts and sighed internally at what she found there.

*ADAM, next time I'm talking to Cheryl Lynn remind me to bring up psychological counseling for those of our people who need it.*

>>**I've made note of your request. May I ask what is wrong?**<<

*All my life, I've always been extremely focused on my goals. So focused that other things going on around me don't affect me the same way something similar would bother a less driven person.*

*Mrs. Jayden here is still suffering from being kidnapped and then displaced from her home and friends. It's not something she chose, but it's something that she's had to accept to ensure the safety of her and her family. And by travelling to Yollin space, we've left everything she's ever known behind.*

*If she's experiencing this level of discontent and uncertainty, I'm sure there must be others who are experiencing those same feelings.*

*I need to talk with Cheryl Lynn about getting counseling for them, or forming support groups or something. For people feeling anxious about their futures to have a place to go and talk things out. It's not something I had considered previously.*

**>>Thank you for the explanation. Should I send her an email on the topic?<<**

*No, thanks. Just remind me. I have a feeling this will be solved more easily if we're face to face and able to bounce ideas off each other.*

"You're going to make me give up Jinx, aren't you?" Anne whispered, wiping a tear from her eye as she talked.

"What? No!" Replied Bethany Anne. "These pups are special. They all decided that it was their right and in their best interests to pick their own people. Jinx has been waiting a long time to find the right person, and she has chosen you. Unless you do something to make her change her mind, you're stuck with her." Bethany Anne tried to school her face to reassure Anne that she was serious.

Jinx gave a questioning little yip.

Anne hugged Jinx tightly while she answered, "No, I

don't want to give you up. I'm happy you chose me! This is the best day *ever*. Well, at least since Bethany Anne and Ashur rescued me from the bad guys who were blackmailing my dad."

"Unless you do that chicken thing again," Sheila had been standing just inside the doorway, listening to the meeting being held in front of her quarters, "I'm not having ..."

A wave of Bethany Anne's hand cut Sheila off middiatribe, not because of a mystical vampiric superpower but by causing Sheila herself to have second thoughts about what could happen if she seriously pissed this woman off.

Bethany Anne looked down at Anne. "How old are you?"

"Sixteen," was Anne's prompt reply.

"Perfect." Bethany Anne smiled. "ADAM, would you please send a brief definition of emancipation to Anne's tablet?"

>>**Done.**<<

"Thank you, ADAM," Bethany Anne replied. "Anne, please get your tablet and read the information ADAM just sent you."

"Now wait just a minute!" Sheila Jayden stormed out to stand in front of Bethany Anne. "You're not taking my child away from me!"

Anne gave Jinx a kiss on the head and headed inside to get her tablet.

"You are quite right. I'm not taking her away from you," Bethany Anne sighed as she faced the upset mother, "but since you're not giving her any options, I am."

Anne had returned to sit beside Jinx as she read. Her voice interrupted the two women. "What exactly does this mean?" Anne asked.

Bethany Anne responded, "Well, you and Jinx wish to be together, correct?" Bethany Anne waited until pup and girl had confirmed her supposition.

"Your mother is basically telling you that it's either her or Jinx, that you can't have both. By signing a statement of emancipation, you are claiming that you are your own person and not subject to your parents' authority anymore. It doesn't mean you don't love your parents, and it doesn't mean you can't see them, unless they choose otherwise. What it does is make you a legal adult at sixteen instead of eighteen. If you wish to go this route, we'll set you up with your own quarters and arrange for you to eat meals in one of the barracks. That way you'll just need to go to school, take care of your laundry, clean your quarters, and work with Jinx."

Anne got to her feet, faced her mother, and took a deep breath. "I'm sorry Mother, but I want Jinx in my life."

"*Fine!*" Sheila Jayden's face turned a very unflattering blotchy red as she vehemently spat, "Just remember when you beg me to allow you to come back home, that *thing* will still not be welcome!" With that, she stormed back into the Jayden family quarters, once again wishing the doors were the old-fashioned kind she could slam behind her.

"ADAM, to make it legal, would you please find the least complicated Emancipation Proclamation and send it to Anne's tablet? Anne, read it through carefully and sign it, if you still wish to do this." Bethany Anne couldn't help but shake her head as she regarded the closed door to Apartment 17.

"Well," Anne started to read through the document ADAM had sent to her tablet, "I can't say I *want* to do this, but Mother has left me no other choice."

>>**Bethany Anne?**<<

*Yes, ADAM.*

>>**Meredith suggests that certain behaviors she has monitored indicate that Tabitha might be currently suffering from depression. Would having Anne live with her until other quarters can be arranged be a good thing for depression or a bad thing?**<<

*ADAM, in this case I think it's a very good idea. Thank you for suggesting it.*

---

*Tabitha?*

The unexpected voice in her head made Tabitha's hand jerk, and she almost dropped the blade she was sharpening. *My Queen?*

There was a quiet chuckle. *How many of us do you have on speed-dial in your head, Ranger Two?*

*Oh, good point. What can I do for your Most Royal Majesty?* Tabitha grinned. She spent a lot of time and effort inventing nicknames for Barnabas, but she didn't get the chance to tweak Bethany Anne very often.

*My Most Royal Majesty is going to remind you about Saint Payback if you don't quit with the crap.*

Having seen the results of the Saint on numerous occasions, Tabitha decided this might be a case of discretion over tweaking. *What did you need, Bethany Anne?*

*Better! Meet me at your quarters in about twenty minutes. I need a service from you.*

*Twenty minutes, Majesty. See you then.*

---

Bethany Anne put an arm around Anne's shoulder and gave her a side hug. "Is there anything here you absolutely can't do without right now?"

Anne tilted her head to look up at Bethany Anne as she pondered the question. "I'm going to need a change of clothes and my school supplies..."

Bethany Anne indicated the Jayden residence with a quick twitch of her head. "We can scrounge up something for you to sleep in, then get you some new clothes tomorrow. Is there anything else you need that's important enough to face your mother for?"

Jinx yipped, and Anne started to laugh. "Jinx just said that humans are silly for not having enough fur to keep ourselves warm."

Bethany Anne grinned at them both, quietly thankful that Jinx was already helping her person deal with the shock she must be suffering. "Come on, let's catch the tram. What do you know about my Rangers?"

---

"You only have two Rangers right now, yes?" Anne asked Bethany Anne as they arrived at one of the tram stops.

"Yes," Bethany Anne confirmed, "and Tabitha came back from her last operation in kind of a funk. So," she looked at Anne and Jinx conspiratorially, "I'm going to ask her to help you two get settled. This way she'll have something to feel good about, and it will hopefully keep her mind off whatever is bothering her. Just don't let her know, okay?" Just then, the tram glided to a silent stop and the two people and the puppy got on.

"I won't … Say anything, that is," Anne agreed once the humans were seated, "but what am I going to tell my dad?"

While telling Anne about Barnabas and Tabitha on the walk to the tram stop Bethany Anne had pondered the same thing, so she wasn't totally unprepared when the question was directed at her. "Well, there are some good things that go with being Queen. One is, I don't have to ask for permission to use video from Meredith's monitoring systems, so I'll have her send your father a copy of everything that happened this afternoon. I'll also enclose a note saying that I think your mother is suffering a lot of emotional turmoil right now, which I believe is probably the largest contributing factor to her current behavior."

"Do you really think that's it?" Anne asked, a glimmer of hope in her eyes.

"I'm going to tell you something, but I want you to promise you will keep it to yourself." Bethany Anne put a finger to her lips as she spoke.

At Anne's nod, she continued, "One of the things I can do if I really have to is read minds. It's kind of gross and I don't do it often, but I *can* do it if I need to. When your mom went ballistic on you, I did a quick read on her. One thing I found out is that she really doesn't like dogs. The other is that she feels resentful you guys ended up here. She'd much rather be back in Las Vegas, minus the kidnappers, of course. And, because she feels way out of control, she's been taking it out on you, since ..."

"I'm something she can control." Anne finished for her.

Bethany Anne pointed a finger at the young woman. "Got it in one. I'm going to see if we, and by we I mean me and the people helping me, can get your mother and others who may be suffering the same issues some sort of professional help."

"You mean, like a shrink?" Anne queried.

"I'm pretty sure they don't like that term, but yes, like a shrink. Or maybe start something like AA, where they form a group and meet up to support each other." The tram's stopping at another station curtailed any further conversation as Bethany Anne led Ashur, Bellatrix, Anne and Jinx down a corridor towards Tabitha's place.

# CHAPTER THREE

Tabitha spent fifteen of the twenty minutes picking up around her place. She lived alone, and wasn't always the neatest person. She had asked Meredith to let her know when Bethany Anne arrived. She was pondering what sort of service her queen could want, and what the hell sort of term "service" was anyway, when Meredith announced Bethany Anne's arrival.

Tabitha opened her door, looked at her guests, blinked, and looked again. No, she decided, she wasn't seeing things. Her friend and Queen was walking up to her place with two adult dogs, a young woman, and a puppy.

Tabitha stepped out of her doorway and greeted Ashur. "Hey, Fuzzball!" "Everyone, come on in," she told the group, and led the way into her main sitting area. "Can I get anyone anything?" she asked.

Ashur came over and pushed his head against Tabitha's leg to encourage her to scratch behind his ears. Bellatrix flopped on the floor as Bethany Anne and Anne settled into chairs, and the puppy sat on the young woman's feet.

Tabitha studied the girl and guessed she was somewhere in her early to mid-teens. She noted the girl sat forward to pet the pup's head.

The puppy looked at Tabitha and asked for some water.

"Do you have a bowl or something to put it in?" Bethany Anne asked as she facepalmed, realizing that they'd need dishes and food for Jinx. "Meredith, could you inform Yelena that Jinx has found her person, and ask her to load a hover cart with food and dishes, please. We'll need that stuff here once she's done. Thanks."

"I'll take care of it, Bethany Anne." Meredith's acknowledgment floated out of the inset ceiling speakers.

"What can I do for you, BA?" Tabitha asked. She had returned from the kitchen and set a bowl of water on the floor in front of the puppy, who was apparently named Jinx.

"Have you been keeping up with the doings of our K9 population?" Bethany Anne asked in return.

"Not really," Tabitha admitted. "Why?"

Bethany Anne shifted in her seat, getting more comfortable.

"I'll keep it short," she began. "The Cliffs Notes version is that Bellatrix and Ashur's pups decided they were going to find their own people as opposed to having people pick them. Jinx has decided that she wants Anne for her person. Mrs. Jayden, the mother of Anne here," Bethany Anne nodded in Anne's direction, "has not adapted well to life on *Meredith Reynolds*, and she doesn't like dogs. The only way I could think of to resolve the situation that didn't require some form of compulsion was to have Anne declare her independence from her family. But, I don't think she's quite ready to live on her own. I was hoping that you could serve as a big sister and help her develop the skills required to live on her own, or be a shoulder she can cry on, if it comes to that."

Tabitha nodded. "I can do that, but where is her stuff?"

"It's an indication of just how bad the situation was at her home that I just told her to leave everything behind. The only thing she possesses is her tablet, and that's because she needed it to read and confirm the emancipation." Bethany Anne shook her head at the memory of Anne's mother's reaction. "Lend her something to sleep in tonight, then take her shopping tomorrow. She'll need clothing, toiletries, and well, basically everything. Charge it to my account. ADAM can confirm that, if any of the merchants give you grief."

"Sounds simple enough. What do we do if you have work for me?" Tabitha asked Bethany Anne.

"Oh, I *will* have work for you. I've got some …umm …" Bethany Anne looked at Anne and sputtered to a stop. "Let's just say there are some beings who are a waste of genetic material … Oh, shut up!" Bethany Anne glared at Tabitha, who was holding her abdomen with one arm while covering her mouth with the other as she tried very hard not to laugh at her Queen.

"I… I can't help … it!" Tabitha got out before her efforts to restrain her merriment failed completely. She crossed both arms on her stomach as she rocked back and forth.

Jinx and Anne looked at each other, wondering what sort of demented person Bethany Anne was sticking them with. "What's wrong with her?" Anne finally asked.

A voice came from the ceiling speakers again. "Bethany

Anne can teach a sailor how to cuss, and I'm guessing Tabitha is finding it very amusing to watch her Queen trying not to be a bad influence on the younger ears present."

Tabitha pointed to the ceiling and nodded her head, still hugging herself because she was laughing so hard it was starting to hurt.

"Any more from you, TOM, and I'll knock some holes in the roof of the doghouse before I kick your ass back out there," Bethany Anne threatened her resident alien.

"Wait!" Jinx cut into the conversation. "You have houses for dogs? That's great, are they big enough for my human to live in too?"

Bethany Anne rolled her eyes, then looked at Jinx. "No, and no," she answered. "Dog houses were something people on Earth would build for their pets to have a place to get out of the weather when they were left in the yard outside. And they were small. I don't know exactly how it began, but it became a saying, usually something a wife directed at her misbehaving husband, that he could sleep outside with the dog. When TOM annoys me too much, I relegate him to an imaginary doghouse."

"Yes," the voice came from the speakers once again. "I know how I'm doing with Bethany Anne by my imaginary sleeping arrangements. Once when I was especially help-ful, I was rewarded with a bedroom all to myself."

Bethany Anne nodded, a small smile for good times remembered showing briefly on her lips. She addressed Tabitha, who had finally gotten her laughter under control.

"As much as I'd love to stick around and entertain you some more, I really need to get back to work." Bethany

Anne couldn't repress the sigh that came with the reminder of the time and effort required to run the Etheric Empire. "I don't expect to need your services as a Ranger for at least a couple weeks yet, so you got this covered?" She asked, looking at Tabitha.

Tabitha turned from Bethany Anne to Anne and Jinx. "We good?"

Anne nodded and Jinx yipped her approval.

Tabitha looked back at Bethany Anne. "We're good, don't worry. I got this," she reassured her Queen.

Bethany Anne rose to her feet and went to give Anne a hug. Since she wasn't a hugger it was a little awkward, but she figured the young woman needed all the support she could get right now.

"After you get settled, research dog houses for Jinx," Bethany Anne suggested as she released Anne. "Thanks, Number Two," she said to Tabitha, then took a step and disappeared.

Anne gazed at the now-vacant spot. "That's so fucking awesome. I really need to learn how to do that." Anne glanced at Tabitha, who was once again howling with laughter, and then at Jinx. "What?"

Once she had managed to calm down again, Tabitha showed Anne and Jinx to the spare bedroom. She and Anne began to make the bed while they waited for Meredith to get Jinx' supplies to the apartment.

"Do you want to talk about it?" Tabitha inquired.

"How much do you know about the trophy wife episode?" Anne asked Tabitha in reply.

"Umm, not a lot," Tabitha admitted. "Didn't BA rescue some family where the dad..." Tabitha trailed off, seeing

Anne nod her head. "My super-ranger deductive powers lead me to guess that you guys were that family."

"Yeah, and the only way that dad could figure out to keep us safe and make sure it didn't happen again was to join up with Bethany Anne's group." Anne continued the story. "My mother, however, wasn't very happy giving up the country club life in Las Vegas to live in a spaceship, and now a space rock. Not enough spas and tennis courts to hang out at here."

"Well, that would be a... *Oh*, I get it." Tabitha had initially wondered why would anyone waste space on a Leviathan-class battleship for tennis courts.

"Yeah," Anne shrugged, "so my dad is happy as a pig in shit because he's now doing what he loves to do for the 'good guys.'" Anne put air quotes around good guys. "But Mother is no longer a big fish in a little pond, and she hasn't adjusted well. And they say *I'm* the one with growing pains and teenage angst and..." Anne broke off as Jinx pushed against her leg and reached up to lick the hand Anne had clenched at her side.

Jinx stood still, not quite knowing what to do for her person, who seemed to be very sad all of a sudden. When Anne slid down to sit on the floor, Jinx wanted to say something, but she had no idea what was happening. She just sat next to Anne, leaning as much of her body as possible against the young human.

Jinx was surprised when Anne suddenly put both arms around her neck and buried her face in Jinx' fur. Jinx looked up at Tabitha, who was standing there silently looking down at Anne. Tabitha made the funny shoulder movement that Jinx had learned was the human way of saying they didn't know.

"Do I need to go back and bite your mother?" Jinx asked.

"No, that's not a good idea, and Bethany Anne said Mother is the way she is because she has some issues that haven't been addressed." Anne raised her head from Jinx' fur and wiped her eyes. "It's just not fair that they think I'm goofing off when I'm trying as hard as I can. I can't control the 'growing pains,' as my parents call them."

Tabitha sat on the bed and put a hand on Anne's shoulder. "I know I'm more your roommate than a parent figure, but I'd still like to see you do well in school. If you need any help you can't get from your friends, let me know and I'll see what I can do."

"Friends! That's a laugh," Anne said forlornly. "I get grounded so often I can't make friends cuz I'm stuck in my room."

Tabitha looked quizzically at Anne. "When was the last time you were grounded?"

"This afternoon, same time I was sent to bed without supper," Anne replied sorrowfully.

"*Puta*! Oh shit, you didn't hear that. Oh, you didn't hear me say 'shit' either." Tabitha went from angry to flustered.

Anne started to giggle. "I've heard them all before and I know what those words mean, so you don't have to worry about saying them around me."

"Deal," Tabitha told her. "Just don't tell anyone else you heard me saying them! Bethany Anne has a way of making a person pay if they upset her, and a new collection of bruises really isn't on my wish list right now."

"Ouch, really?" Anne tilted her head back to look up at Tabitha.

"Ouch, really!" Tabitha winced. "Bethany Anne believes that pain is a great motivator. The bigger the lesson she feels you need to be taught, the more a sparring session with her hurts. Don't get me wrong, she won't just pop in from nowhere and start beating on you. She even gives the bad guys a chance to surrender. But once you've gone past a certain point, Bethany Anne lets pain be the teacher. Unless you're just a douche bag; then she simply removes you from the equation. Now, did I hear you say you didn't get any supper?"

"Yup, you did. I wasn't properly cowed by being grounded for the umpteenth time, so it was 'off to bed without supper for you, young lady.'" Anne giggled some more while she waved her hand and affected an English accent, like a queen passing judgment on the peons.

"Well, I spent a lot of time hungry while I was growing up, and I can absolutely say that it doesn't do anything positive as far as a person's performance is concerned," Tabitha told Anne. "I don't have anything here to eat right now, but we can hit up the Guardians' mess. Weres are constantly hungry, so their mess always has some sort of food available."

"I could eat a bowl of soup, if they have any," Anne admitted.

"If they don't, I'm sure they can thaw some or open a can or…something," Tabitha promised. "Let's head out."

---

The room that Tabitha took Anne and Jinx to was fairly quiet since it was past normal supper hours, but, as promised, there was food in a few hot pans. Having been set up primarily to feed Weres, the selection tended toward proteins, but Anne wasn't interested in gnawing on a steak.

Jinx, however, was very excited by all the wonderful smells coming from just above her head.

"You're one of the Rangers, right?" A middle-aged woman in a chef's uniform and hairnet pushed through the swinging doors from the kitchen.

"Yes I am, but we're here so this young lady can get some soup or something. She hasn't had supper yet," Tabitha informed the chef.

The woman looked Anne over carefully. "Not a Were?" She guessed.

"Nope, straight-up human, but we do have a modified K-9 with us," Anne replied, pointing to Jinx.

"*Wow*! Which of you is the lucky person to get one of Ashur's puppies?" The chef asked, kneeling down and putting out a hand toward Jinx.

Jinx sniffed her hand and then allowed the chef-person to scratch her under the chin. *Oh, that felt really good!*

"This is Jinx, and she decided she wanted to see what life with a teenager was like. She chose me, just earlier today," Anne replied with a smile.

"The Ranger said you want ..."

"It's Tabitha. My name's Tabitha, not Ranger," Tabitha interrupted the chef.

"Tabitha, okay. Tabitha said something about soup?" The chef asked Anne.

"Yes, please, if possible. And my name's Anne. I understand that people-food is not good as a constant diet for dogs, but could we get a piece of steak for Jinx?"

The chef nodded her assent, then asked, "Chicken noodle soup do?"

"That would be wonderful. And a piece of bread or a roll with it, if possible," Anne agreed.

The chef smiled and turned toward the kitchen. "One bowl of chicken noodle soup with a slice of Italian bread on the side, and a steak for the pooch, coming right up. You sure you don't want anything, Tabitha? Slice of cheesecake, perhaps?"

"I give!" Tabitha shouted at the chef's receding back. "Who can turn down cheesecake?"

In less than five minutes the chef returned, carrying a tray with bread, soup, and a piece of round steak, along with two slices of cheesecake.

She set the tray on the table that Tabitha and Anne had claimed and passed one of the pieces of cheesecake to Tabitha.

At Tabitha's raised eyebrow, she stated, "You said Anne missed supper, not that you did. Enjoy, everybody."

With that the chef went back to the kitchen, and the faint bangs of pots and pans were heard.

Anne lifted the plate with the steak and looked at Jinx. "I know you are your own dog and you guys are way smarter than normal dogs, but I've seen normal dogs eat steak before and they just choke it down as fast as they can. No one is going to try to take this away from you, so please chew before swallowing."

Jinx, almost dancing in place, yipped her agreement and laid down by the plate Anne set on the floor. Not wanting to disappoint her human, she carefully chewed off a section of the steak and then took her time. "Oh, this is won— Ow, I bit my tongue!" Jinx whined.

"That's why humans have a rule about not talking with their mouths full of food," Anne told the pup, "Not only does it look gross, but you can bite your tongue or cheek or even spew food all over the place. Boys are the absolute worse, cuz they seem to think it's funny to be gross."

Jinx waited until she had swallowed the meat before speaking again. "I can see I have a lot more to learn." She chewed off another piece of steak.

Two humans and one very happy German Shepherd puppy finished their food and returned to Tabitha's apartment.

The hover cart was waiting outside the door with food and dishes for Jinx. The cart was narrow enough that it could fit through the door so Anne just pushed it inside. She followed Tabitha into the kitchen, where Tabitha made room in one of the cupboards for the container of dog food. Tabitha suggested that Anne wash the dishes that were sent for Jinx before she put anything down for the pup. Anne scrubbed them thoroughly then filled the now-clean dishes with food and water.

Tabitha went to her room and found an old sleep-tee she thought would fit Anne well enough for one night. She joined Jinx and Anne in their bedroom and offered the tee to Anne. "Change into this, and I'll set your clothes to wash during the night so you'll have something clean to wear tomorrow."

Anne thanked Tabitha and headed off to the bathroom, returning shortly with her clothes bundled in her arms. "If I understand things correctly, I'm pretty much responsible for myself now, so I guess that means I need to learn how to take care of my own laundry."

"And you will," Tabitha told the young woman as she held out her hands and made a "gimme" motion with her fingers, "just not tonight. You've already had a full day. I'll show you how the laundry works tomorrow after shopping. You'll need to wash everything before you wear it anyway, so you'll get lots of practice."

Anne sighed and handed her dirty clothes to Tabitha, but before she could react, Anne stepped forward and gave the surprised Ranger a hug.

"Thanks for everything," she whispered in Tabitha's ear before releasing her and stepping back.

"*De nada.*" Tabitha hoped the blush she felt on her cheeks wasn't visible. "You and Furbucket get a good sleep."

"Furbucket?" Jinx looked at Tabitha, confusion evident in her voice.

"It's a nickname," Tabitha told the pup. "I call your dad Fuzzball, so you're Furbucket." She stuck out her tongue at Jinx, then turned and headed out of the room.

"I don't know if I like nicknames," Tabitha heard Jinx comment to Anne as she closed the door behind her.

# CHAPTER FOUR

The next morning Tabitha, carrying Anne's cleaned clothes, peeked into Anne's room. The girl was still asleep.

Tabitha smiled as she noticed Jinx curled up behind Anne with her head resting on the girl's hip. Jinx cracked her eyes at the sound of the bedroom door opening.

"Busy day, with all the shopping we're going to need to do," Tabitha told Jinx. "Do you want to wake up Sleeping Beauty, or do you want me to?"

"This Sleeping Beauty, is that another of your nickname things?" Jinx tried to keep the growl out of her voice, but she was beginning to think that she *really* didn't like nicknames.

"Yes and no," Tabitha answered.

Jinx did growl this time. "How can it be both?"

"Well, Sleeping Beauty is sort of standard nickname for females who oversleep, so yes, it's a nickname. But it's not something that I specifically thought up, so no, it's not one of *my* nicknames. Not like Furbucket. That *is* one of mine." Tabitha smiled proudly.

Jinx looked at Tabitha, then smiled in reply. "You might be good at making up names, but I've got the better set of teeth."

Tabitha, who wasn't really used to seeing a dog smiling, was momentarily taken aback at seeing the mouthful of pointed and sharp teeth being displayed for her benefit. She thought Jinx was snarling at her at first. Relieved to realize this wasn't the case, she said the first thing that came to mind. "Bethany Anne has us both beat."

"Ashur's person?"

"Oh, hell yeah," Tabitha replied. "Just wait until you see her go complete vamp sometime! Then you'll see what a real set of chompers looks like. Mind you, even *she* can't beat the Weres in their Pricolici form. Those mothers have a huge set of teeth."

"Mothers? Whose mothers?" Jinx wondered.

"It's using another word as a nickname," Anne groused from under her blanket, "like saying guys, but meaning people, not males. As in, couldn't you guys have been a little quieter?"

"This human language is quite confusing," Jinx declared. "I don't know how Matrix learned it so fast."

"Well, since you're now awake," Tabitha decided to change the subject, "what would you like for breakfast? I'll go to the mess and bring something back for you while you get showered and dressed. We have all that shopping to do today, so we need to get moving."

"Um, French toast with syrup, and a few strips of bacon?" Anne asked hopefully.

"I'm sure that can be arranged. Back in about ten, so get your butt moving!" Tabitha turned and headed out the door. "Oh, and," she stuck her head back into the bedroom, "OJ, or what to drink?"

"Milk would be best, since orange juice can be too acidic for me some mornings," Anne told her as she kicked off the covers.

"Got it. Back in a few." Tabitha's voice floated back into the bedroom as she left on the food run.

Anne enjoyed her French-toast-and-bacon breakfast, and even though she knew it wasn't a good habit to be getting into, she couldn't help but offer Jinx some of the bacon.

Jinx, however, decided bacon should be an important part of every breakfast. She had been smart, though, and had eaten some of her kibble while Anne was taking a shower. Eating the kibble first ensured she would not get hungry while they were out, and also that she wouldn't have to ruin the taste of the bacon by eating kibble afterwards.

Once breakfast was finished, all three of them headed to the main shopping district of the *Meredith Reynolds*.

The multi-level shopping area was not complete yet, because Bethany Anne had asked the base planners to build more shop space than the humans could fill. Having gotten to know and made friends with the Yollins, Bethany Anne had realized that there would be a lot of merchants in Yollin space who would be happy to open stores in the *Meredith Reynolds'* retail court.

It was a testament to universal marketing forces that Meredith and the team of advisers who decided on shop rentals had received more applications than they had shops to rent.

Anne was surprised to see how many aliens were visiting the human shops until she overheard a conversation between a shop owner and one of the Yollins.

"Your best bet," the owner was saying, "would be to contact one of the designers we have on station. For a small fee, I could introduce you to a young lady who is just getting into the business, but don't let her being new put you off. She's very well connected, if you get my meaning. Show her what sort of materials you plan to use. Have her design clothes for humans using them, sell the finished product in your store, and you'll be golden."

"Why would he change to gold?" Jinx whispered to Anne, proving that the puppy had been listening to the conversation as well.

"It's another one of those things people just say. Gold is expensive and is used for money in some places, so saying you're golden just means you'll get rich. At least that's what I think it means," Anne replied, giving Jinx the best answer she could.

"I think I need to go to school with you," Jinx told Anne seriously. "I don't want to be left on my own all day anyway, and it seems like there is so much more I need to learn."

Tabitha, who had been listening in on the conversation, interjected, "That's not a bad idea, but you will have to behave yourself and stay with Anne the whole time she's in classes. Otherwise the teachers will claim you are a distraction and try to make you stay at home."

Jinx stopped and turned to Tabitha. "Why would they do that?" she asked.

"Another old saying is 'old habits die hard.' The teachers

are from Earth, where dogs are normally considered dumb animals. Smart enough to train, but not smart enough to think or talk like a person. Add to that, the fact there are so few of you on the *Meredith Reynolds*. That makes you a novelty, and you're going to get some people thinking that you being in school is too much of a distraction to the other students. If you truly want to go to school with Anne and will behave all day, I'll talk to Bethany Anne and make sure that the school knows it's happening with her approval."

"Good," replied Jinx. "I saw Bethany Anne before when she and Ashur came to visit Yelena and my mom, but I guess I didn't realize that she was the alpha of the humans."

"That's a good way of putting it." Tabitha nodded at Jinx. "Bethany Anne is *definitely* the alpha!"

---

Several stores later, Tabitha ordered a hover cart, from Meredith to carry all the purchases. She was feeling uneasy about Anne, however. The girl was extremely quiet for a teen, and she didn't offer much of an opinion on the clothes they were buying. Knowing it was mean in a way but desperately wanting to break through the girl's shell, Tabitha found a training bra and offered it to Anne. "Here, it looks like this is something you need," she said, wincing internally at the expected outburst.

"Nope, thanks though," Anne replied, lifting both hands to point at her A-cup breasts. "I've got the girls trained already. It's women like you who need the extra help. Mine don't make my tops fit too tightly, and I don't have to worry about them falling out of my bra and embarrassing me. And oh my God, did you see that video where the lady with the D-cups just about knocked a guy out of his chair when she turned too quickly? Those suckers need training. Mine are good, however."

Tabitha stood completely still, trying to get over the shock of Anne's response. Anne, working very hard to not burst out laughing at the gob-smacked look on her face, couldn't help but add, "If you find something pink and lacy in a 32A however, be sure to send it my way." And with that, Anne moved farther into the racks of clothing.

"What? *Wait*!" Tabitha hurried after the young woman. "Where the hell have you been hiding that?" she asked, completely flummoxed by Anne's reaction and answer.

"Hiding what?" Anne asked, not quite sure what Tabitha was asking her.

"We've been shopping half the day and you've hardly said a word about anything we've bought you, but I try to jerk your chain to get a reaction and you cut me off at the knees. *That* what!" Tabitha's Latin nature was coming out, her voice getting louder as she spoke.

"You've got a good taste in clothes, and they're just school clothes anyway. It's not like I'm dating." Anne's nose crinkled in disgust. "I'm not looking for a gown for a formal or a LBD or something else that would require dressing up, so why argue or complain when you're buying me nicer stuff than my mother normally would?" she calmly answered Tabitha like it was the most obvious thing in the world.

When they had finished purchasing all the basics for Anne, Tabitha noticed that the girl didn't seem as energetic as she had at the beginning of the day. Checking with Achronyx, she found it was almost suppertime. "Do you want to have supper in the mess again, or at one of the restaurants here?"

"Don't you ever cook?" Anne asked.

"Sure, scrambled eggs, toaster pastry, tacos, and I can even manage a dish of enchiladas," Tabitha replied glibly.

"Why don't we hit the mess again, but let's stop by your apartment first so you can show me how the washer and dryer work. That way I can get some clothes going while we eat," Anne suggested.

Jinx, who had been slowly moving toward a stand that served hotdogs and bratwursts, yipped a complaint.

Anne looked at Jinx. "You can only have one, and no bun. Do you want a dog or a brat?"

"Dog? They serve dog here? Why does Bethany Anne allo…" Jinx' outrage cooled suddenly as she watched the two humans laughing so hard they were holding onto each other to remain standing. *"What?"* she asked, already suspecting that English, the pesky human language that most the people on the *Meredith Reynolds* spoke, had somehow tripped her again.

"It's a type of sausage, same as the bratwurst. Wait, I'll look it up." During the expedition they had decided to get Anne a new tablet, so she dug around in one of the shopping bags to look for it.

Knowing it most likely wouldn't have a charge, Tabitha pulled her tablet out and offered it to Anne. "Here. Mine is charged."

"Thanks." Anne accepted the tablet and sat at a vacant table in front of the sausage vendor. "Okay," she said, looking at Jinx. "Eeww, gross!" Anne wrinkled her nose in disgust. "Apparently there was a concern a long time ago that they actually contained dog meat, so that might be where they got the name from. They are also called frank-furters or wieners, depending on where they were made and what meat went into them, dog not being normal meat. Generally they are made from pork or beef or a combination of both. In the US where I came from, they also used chicken in them because chicken was cheaper."

"I'm not going to call them dogs," Jinx declared. "So what's the difference between a frankfarter and a brat?"

Anne grabbed her midsection and doubled over laughing.

"What now?" Jinx wondered.

"It's frank*furter*," Tabitha answered the pup. "A fart is something else altogether, and I don't want to discuss that here."

Jinx looked back and forth between Tabitha and Anne. "Can I have a brat then? The other thing doesn't sound very good."

Tabitha nodded and bought two brats and one bun from the vendor, then broke the one in the bun in half and handed part of it to Anne. "So we don't get too hungry while we go home to start laundry," she offered in explana-tion. She blew on the other brat so Jinx wouldn't burn herself.

"Would you break it into pieces, please?" Jinx asked. "I don't want to chew off a piece and have the rest fall on the floor."

"Oh, good thinking," Tabitha agreed. "Would it gross you out to know that normal Earth dogs wouldn't care if it was on the floor?" she asked as she went back to the vendor to request a disposable plate.

Jinx looked at Anne. "She's not pulling that joke thing again, is she?" Jinx shuddered with disgust.

"I'm afraid not," Tabitha said as she returned and put the plate with the cut-up brat on the floor.

Jinx sniffed at the pieces before giving one a cautious lick. "Don't say anything more about it. I want to enjoy this without having yucky pictures in my head."

It didn't take any of them long to finish eating their snack, then they all headed back to Tabitha's apartment.

CHAPTER FIVE

The next day was Sunday, and it was spent quietly at the apartment. Anne laundered and put away all her new clothes while she charged her new tablet. About midday, the apartment's EI announced a visitor. Anne was closest to the door, so she yelled "Want me to get that?" toward Tabitha's room.

"You live here too, so go ahead." Tabitha's reply floated down the hallway.

Anne keyed the door open and froze, momentarily shocked.

"Hi, baby girl. May I come in for a minute?" her dad asked.

Anne reflexively started to move aside, but stopped and threw herself into her father's arms instead as tears rolled down her face. Jinx pressed up against her leg to offer what support she could to her human. Between her dad's big hug and Jinx pushing against her leg while whining slightly, Anne finally got herself under control and stepped back. She reached down and scratched behind Jinx' ear. "I'm okay, girl, thanks," she told the pup. "Hiya, Daddy. Come on in," Anne invited, walking inside so Jinx and her father could follow.

"Who is it?" Tabitha asked, coming into the sitting area of the apartment.

Remembering her manners, Anne said, "Tabitha, this is my dad, Mason. Daddy, this is Bethany Anne's Number Two Ranger, Tabitha. The German Shepherd is from Ashur and Bellatrix, and her name is Jinx. Jinx, as you heard, this is my dad. Unfortunately he doesn't have the newest implant, so he won't be able to understand you."

Mason Jayden shook hands with Tabitha and took the seat she offered him. "How is it you can understand Jinx without an implant?" he inquired.

"Dunno." Anne shrugged. "I just can. I could understand Ashur way back when he and Bethany Anne rescued us."

"The dogs really are talking, and Anne can actually understand what they are saying?" Mason asked Tabitha.

Jinx started to growl, and Tabitha reached out and put a hand on the girl's arm, sensing an imminent outburst from the teen. "Unless you are willing to believe what your daughter is telling you, I expect this will be a short conversation," Tabitha advised Anne's father.

"Sorry," Mason said to Tabitha, "but this just seems so science fiction-y."

"First, you need to direct your apology to your daughter. Second, we're light years from Earth in alien space living in a hollowed-out asteroid, and you worry that your daughter being able to talk to the dogs is science fiction?" Tabitha looked so incredulous that Anne started to giggle at her expression.

"Well, considering everything that has happened over the past couple of years, I guess you have a point," Mason acknowledged.

Tabitha sat back contentedly and observed father and daughter reconnecting in a way that had obviously been missing for a while. She was especially interested in how Jinx seemed to be able to help Anne deal with her emotions. Every time Anne got upset or overwhelmed, Jinx pushed against her leg, put her head in Anne's lap, or did something else to subtly change Anne's focus. At one point Tabitha made some nachos, and the next two hours passed quickly.

Finally Mason stood. "I need to be getting back to your mother. I didn't tell her I was coming to visit because I didn't want her to think I'd chosen sides."

"That's okay, Daddy. I'll miss you and Mom, but I have Tabitha and Jinx to help me. Mom really needs your support right now because she doesn't have anyone else. Maybe we can meet occasionally at the food court or somewhere we could get a burger or something." Anne was surprised at how much calmer she felt, knowing her dad didn't hate her for something she had no control over.

"Sounds like a plan, baby girl," her father replied. He gave her a big hug and headed home, hoping with all his heart that his wife would be able to adapt and learn to accept the life they now led.

The next morning, Anne and Jinx got up quietly. After a quick shower, Anne made sure there was food and water for Jinx and grabbed herself one of the protein shakes she and Tabitha had bought the day before. By the time the two needed to head for school, there was still no sign of Tabitha.

"Let's go, Jinx," Anne said to her canine companion. "I don't want to be late on the first day that I'm responsible for myself."

Being one of only seven dogs on the QBBS *Meredith Reynolds*, Jinx attracted a lot of attention on the tram ride to Anne's school.

Anne quickly became tired of explaining. "No, she didn't purchase Jinx," "No, she wasn't selling Jinx," and "No, she didn't know how the pups chose their companions."

Jinx herself rapidly got tired of everyone wanting to "pet the puppy." These humans didn't have a standard action that went with the word "pet." To some, it meant running their hands down Jinx' back, which she didn't mind. Others patted her sides, which was mildly uncomfortable but tolerable. One of the smaller humans seemed to think it meant pulling her ears, which she really didn't like.

Anne sensed Jinx' discomfort with the boy's yanking, so she reached out, grabbed the boy's ear, and pulled it. The boy started crying, and his mother snatched him away.

"What the hell do you think you're doing?" The irate mother snarled at Anne.

"I was teaching him that having your ears pulled isn't a nice thing," Anne calmly told the mother. Anne put out a hand to stop Jinx, who had gotten to her feet and was starting to growl at the woman. "Your son was hurting Jinx the way he was pulling on her ears. You apparently didn't feel a need to correct his actions, so I showed him what having an ear pulled felt like. Jinx was getting to the point where *she* wanted to show him what having his ears pulled felt like, but since she doesn't have hands or fingers, she would have pulled his ear with her teeth. If you're going to ask someone to let your son pet their dog, you need to be responsible for making sure your boy isn't hurting it."

"He's just a child!" The woman huffed.

"Exactly," Anne responded. "And as the adult, it's your job to teach him the difference between petting and hurting. Since you weren't willing to do that, you left it to me, and now he knows that pulling ears isn't fun or appropriate."

"Who is your mother?" The woman asked. "I'm going to have a talk with her about your attitude!"

Anne pulled her tablet from her backpack and keyed in a number.

"Do you know what time it is?" said an irritated voice from her tablet.

"Yes, Ranger Tabitha, I'm aware of the time. I'm sorry I had to wake you, but I'm having issues on the tram to school." Anne figured she'd better get right to the point.

The woman had set her son down while Anne was calling Tabitha, and he hid behind her leg. This left her hands free, and she snatched Anne's tablet.

*Well, I can see why the kid's a brat*, Anne thought to herself.

"Are you this girl's mother?" The woman asked. "She attacked my son!"

"Nope, not her mother. I'm Ranger Tabitha, and I'm Anne's roommate and role model."

"What kind of role model teaches a girl to attack a child?" The woman hissed at Tabitha.

"Anne, what's going on?" Tabitha asked, her voice sounding a little tinny coming from the tablet's speakers.

"This woman asked if her son could pet Jinx, but instead of petting, he started pulling Jinx' ears. He was pulling on them hard enough that I could almost feel her pain. The mother wasn't doing anything about his behavior, and instead of letting Jinx bite him, I reached out and gave him a tug on the ear so he could understand how it felt. I didn't tug that hard, but he started to cry, so his mother got mad at me and demanded to talk to my mother. Instead of trying to explain my home situation, I called you," Anne explained to Tabitha.

"Just a minute." Tabitha told them, then asked the station's EI, "Meredith, you have video on all the trams, right?" They couldn't hear Meredith's reply, but then they heard Tabitha again. "Can you show me the last five minutes of video from the tram Anne is on?" Three minutes later she said, "That's enough, Meredith, thanks. Okay, lady, even on the video I can tell that Anne didn't really do anything strong enough to hurt your kid. He's just pissed that someone expected him to behave. Now, as a Queen's Ranger I can investigate this further if you want, but if I do that and find that your son is at fault ..."

"That won't be necessary," the woman cut Tabitha off. She grabbed her son's hand and started towards the opposite end of the tram.

"Hey, my tablet!" Anne called to the woman's back.

The very upset lady spun and threw the tablet at Anne, who managed to catch it before it hit the floor.

"I wonder if Bethany Anne could enact a law to require people to get a license to have kids?" Anne heard Tabitha mumble as the connection was closed.

Jinx stayed pressed against Anne's leg as they exited the tram for the short walk to the school.

---

"What do you think you're doing, Miss Jayden?" Asked the teacher who was monitoring the main entrance to the school.

"Umm, coming to school?" Anne replied, somewhat confused.

The teacher pointed at Jinx. "And why do you think you can bring a dog to school?"

---

Tabitha had been in the middle of a really nice dream. Sun, sand and beefcake guys everywhere, when Anne had called about her problem with the lady and her bratty kid. Hoping to continue her dream, she tried to get back to sleep after she terminated the call. She'd finally gotten into a comfortable position and was just drifting off when her tablet rang again. *"Hijo de puta*, does Achronyx have a camera somewhere to let you know I'm still in bed?" she grumped as she answered the call.

"I don't know about any bugs he might have access to, but he's not asking me to call you. I'm at school, and they won't let Jinx into class with me," Anne stated.

"So?" Tabitha asked when Anne didn't continue.

"You mentioned you would talk with Bethany Anne about permission ..."

"*Joder! Mierda!*" Tabitha's outburst cut off Anne's explanation. This one was on her. She *had* said she'd talk with Bethany Anne, and she had totally forgotten to do it. "Hang tight, Anne. Sorry, my bad."

*Bethany Anne?*

*In a meeting. It'll take about three minutes to wrap it up,* Bethany Anne replied.

Deciding more sleep was not in her future this morning, Tabitha got out of bed and headed for her kitchen to make some coffee. She was just taking her first cautious sip of the hot black elixir when Bethany Anne got back to her.

*Okay, what's up? You sounded quite formal. Are you sick or something?*

*No, but I goofed and now Anne is left holding the bag, so to speak. Jinx decided that she should go to classes with Anne, and I told them that I'd clear it with you so the school would be all right with it,* Tabitha confessed.

*You're doing that now, what's the issue?* Bethany Anne wanted to know.

*Anne and Jinx are being refused entry to the school because I didn't have this conversation with you a couple of days ago.* Bethany Anne could hear the whine in Tabitha's mental voice.

*Should I ask how you managed that?* Bethany Anne replied.

Tabitha cringed slightly. *Truth is, Anne's a good kid, we had lots of fun shopping, and I simply forgot.*

*Easy enough to fix. I'll have Cheryl Lynn contact the school and take care of it. Anything else?*

*Thanks, boss, and nope, that's it for now,* Tabitha informed her Queen. Tabitha managed to imbibe her first sip of coffee, now cool enough it didn't burn her mouth, and headed for the shower to get her day started.

---

Anne had moved away from the door and set her backpack on the ground, and proceeded to use it as a seat as she propped her back against the wall of the school. Anne threw one arm across Jinx' shoulders as the puppy leaned against her. She felt Jinx tense slightly as a pair of shoes and legs appeared in front of her. Tilting her head back, Anne looked up to see the school's principal and quickly scrambled to her feet. "Sir?" She asked.

"What's with you and the dog, Miss Jayden?" The principal asked.

Jinx, who had stood when Anne did, growled.

The principal, who had the latest Etheric Empire implant heard, "Maybe someone should ask the dog!" He looked down, face showing his shock. "Excuse me, young lady, young GSD, why don't we move this conversation to my office?" The principal stepped into the doorway, creating a break in the stream of students that were arriving for class. Anne and Jinx slid into that empty space and followed the principal through the doors and into the hallways. Once everyone was settled in the office, the principal looked at the human and canine females sitting in front of him and asked, "Okay, who wants to start this conversation?"

"Me," Jinx replied promptly. "Once I had chosen Anne

as my partner, I became involved in a lot more human conversations, and people were using numerous words I didn't understand. It made sense to me that instead of sitting at home all day I should come to school with Anne so that I would learn more words and information, so I told Ranger Tabitha that I'd like to take classes with Anne. She said it was a good idea, and she'd talk to my dad's person about it. This has been the first school day since Anne and I bonded. Here we are."

The principal looked back and forth between the girl and the dog. "Well that would explain the call from the Empress' personal assistant," the principal murmured.

This started a long conversation where the logistics and rules of Jinx being in school with Anne were discussed. Jinx was to stick to Anne like glue except during PE class, when she would sit or lie in front of the bleachers where both Anne and Jinx could always have each other in sight. Once all the details had been worked out, the principal sent all the teachers and Anne an email acknowledging the presence of Jinx and the expected behavior of the two students.

# CHAPTER SIX

Tabitha looked confused. "What do you mean?"

"I learned it in school this week. Dogs have two hundred million more scent receptors than humans. Even compared to the vampires' and Weres' improved senses, dogs can smell things humans just can't."

"Oookkaaayy." Tabitha dragged the word out while she thought about what she'd just heard. "What does that have to do with this?"

"Because I've been around all those other young humans for the past few days, I've been able to determine the common smells. All humans have a smell that says 'human.' All Yollins have a smell that says 'Yollin.' The other aliens that I have scented on the base all have unique smells that identify them by race, too. And then, each individual has their own scent.

"If you were to give me a shirt and ask me who wore it, I would smell it and tell you the wearer was human, then sniff it again for other odors and narrow it down to

Tabitha. I've smelled hundreds of young people this week, and they all smell human and then have individual scents."

"My person has an extra scent that I don't smell on any of the others, and it's yucky. I remembered a conversation that Mom's person had one time about therapy dogs—dogs that were trained to know the smell of bad things happening to their people. Anne has an extra smell like that, and I think it means she's sick. That would explain why she's tired all the time. What do we do?" Jinx' ears drooped at this question. "I don't want to lose my person!"

"How sure of this are you?" Tabitha asked, concerned at Jinx' attitude.

"Of the smell? One hundred percent," Jinx assured Tabitha. "Of what it means? No idea. I'm just guessing, based on the smell itself. Like I said, it's yucky. I was willing to put up with it to be with my person, but now I'm sure it's not normal. Something is wrong!"

Tabitha held up her hands to calm Jinx. "I believe you, just give me a moment to think about this," she told the distressed dog.

*Boss Lady?*

*What do you need, Tabitha?* Bethany Anne responded right away.

*Sorry to bother you. I'm having a conversation with Jinx, and she feels pretty sure that there is something wrong with Anne. Jinx says that Anne has an odor to her that the other humans at the school don't have, and she thinks it might be a disease. Poor Jinx seems pretty stressed out by it. I was wondering if we could stick Anne in the Pod-doc for a diagnosis, just to see what's going on with her.*

*We don't have anyone in it right now, so I don't see why not,*

Bethany Anne sent. *Bring her by TOM's ship tomorrow and we'll stuff her in and see what it says.*

*Great! Thanks, Bethany Anne, I'll tell Jinx. Hopefully that will make her feel better. What time tomorrow?* Tabitha remembered to ask before ending the conversation.

*ADAM says I have ten hundred free.*

*Oh, praise God,* Tabitha sent to Bethany Anne, *a civilized time of the day. See you then, and thank you.*

*Ten tomorrow, see you then,* Bethany Anne replied before the quiet in her head told Tabitha that Bethany Anne was no longer in contact.

She squatted and gave Jinx a hug. "Don't worry. I talked with Bethany Anne, and she is going to put Anne in the original Kurtherian Pod-doc on TOM's ship. It's the most advanced medical tool we have, and if there is something wrong with Anne, the Pod-doc will find out what it is. Chances are excellent it will be able to treat it. You just need to help me get Anne up and moving tomorrow, because we need to meet Bethany Anne at ten in the morning."

"I still have trouble understanding human time. Just come tell me when you want her, and I'll make sure she gets up even if I have to lick her feet to do it."

Tabitha laughed at Jinx' wrinkled nose. "Better you than me."

The next morning Tabitha stuck her head in Anne's bedroom, and couldn't help but smile at the sight. Anne was curled up on her side, and Jinx was curled nose to tail against the small of Anne's back. At the sound of the door, Jinx stood and stretched, then shook herself and looked at Tabitha. "It's that time," said Tabitha. Jinx nodded that she understood, so Tabitha closed the door and headed for the kitchen to make coffee.

Jinx took a moment to decide the best way to accomplish the goal of getting Anne up and ready for the day. She decided her first attack would be the covers. She pawed at the sheet by Anne's shoulder until there was enough wrinkle to grab it with her mouth, then started tugging it toward the foot of the bed, taking the blanket with it. At the bottom of the bed Jinx had to let go and jump to the floor. From there she grabbed the bedding again and pulled it all the way off.

"Stop it," Anne mumbled, her hand feeling for covers that were no longer there.

Jinx jumped back on the bed and gave Anne's nose a quick lick. "You need to get up!" She told the drowsy girl. "We're going to go visit my dad and Bethany Anne."

"What?" Anne sat up and rubbed her eyes. "What are you talking about?"

"After you fell asleep yesterday, Tabitha was talking with Bethany Anne, and we're all going to get together this morning," Jinx told her, intentionally leaving out the reason for the meeting.

"Oh. Okay," Anne stretched and sat up on the edge of the bed. "What time?"

"We are meeting them at ten."

Anne looked at her tablet and saw it was eight-thirty. "Great," she said, "I've got time for a shower."

Thirty minutes later, Anne had showered and dressed. She wandered into the kitchen and smiled when she saw that Tabitha had put on a kettle so Anne could make a cup of tea. Lately she was finding that tea was easier on her stomach than coffee. She fed Jinx while her tea was steeping, and five minutes later sat at the table with a cup of tea and a toaster waffle. "So, what's the deal?" She asked Tabitha.

Tabitha was a Queen's Ranger for a reason, and she immediately deduced that Jinx had kept Anne ignorant of the details related to the outing. "I was talking with Bethany Anne yesterday about how much better a dog's sense of smell is compared to a human's, and we're going to get together and see if that information would be of any benefit to the Etheric Empire." Tabitha made up the best excuse she could on short notice.

"Oh? What were you thinking?" Anne asked, between bites of her waffle.

"Jinx mentioned that certain therapy dogs could smell stuff that humans had no way of knowing was a problem, so we're wondering just how much this sort of talent could be useful," Tabitha replied, trying to keep the conversation truthful without divulging the real reason for the meeting. She checked the time and was very relieved to find out that they needed to be leaving if they were to meet Bethany Anne on time. "Let's head out," she said to Anne. "Unfortunately, the Queen has a lot of shit to do during her days, and she only has an hour to meet with us."

"I wonder if she realized how much of her personal life she was going to lose before she decided to try to save the world from aliens?" Anne commented as she followed Tabitha out of their apartment.

Tabitha looked over her shoulder at the younger woman. "Honestly? I doubt it. I don't think anyone could have comprehended the scope of the job back then. Hell, even though Bethany Anne knew that the goal was to fight aliens, we were so busy just trying to rid Earth of the Forsaken that I doubt she had any idea at all where she'd end up.

"Wow!" Anne exclaimed. "How long have you been with Bethany Anne?"

Tabitha looked embarrassed as she answered, "I had been forced to work for the bad guys, and BA took two of us captive on the second op after she'd been changed."

"Wait!" Anne said. "Was that the Miami op? We learned about that in school. Holy shit, you're old enough to be history!"

Tabitha looked at the young woman walking with her. "And you, smartass, are part of the infamous trophy wife operation. Who do you think will get more exposure as time goes by?"

"You will," Anne replied to the older woman, "but more because you're Ranger Two than because of the Miami situation."

"Well, you're one of seven people in the Etheric Empire to have a dog choose you, so I think the jury is still out on which of us might become the more famous." Tabitha stuck her tongue out at Anne at the end of her sentence.

Anne was trying very hard not to laugh, but a giggle escaped. "Way to be the adult in this conversation, Tabs."

"Tabitha, not Tabs! Ranger Tabitha sounds official. Not necessarily badass, but official. Ranger Tabs sounds like something from a kids' TV show," Tabitha grumped.

Anne smiled at Tabitha, then rushed forward when she saw Bethany Anne and Ashur waiting at a doorway. "Ashur!" She shouted as she dropped to her knees and slid forward to greet the big male. She then reached over to hug Jinx, who had come up to her sire to bump noses. "I don't love you any less," she whispered to Jinx, "but I'll always have a soft spot for Ashur."

Jinx turned and slurped her tongue across Anne's cheek to indicate that she didn't hold any grudge against Anne for liking Ashur as much as she did.

"What's up with Anne?" Bethany Anne asked the others.

"Huh?" Anne looked around, confusion evident by her expression.

"She doesn't smell right," Jinx declared. Jinx turned to Ashur, "It's faint, but if you pay attention to the odors, you'll catch a scent that isn't found on other humans."

Ashur stood up and meticulously sniffed Anne. He trotted down the hallway to get to a busier corridor and stood there as several humans walked by. He carefully checked their scents, then returned to Anne and sniffed her one more time. "I smell it," he told Jinx. "I never realized it was different before."

Jinx looked at her dad and then at Anne as she answered, "I noticed it right away, but I didn't understand it wasn't normal until I started going to school with Anne and had all the other young humans to compare her to. When I heard someone talking about how therapy dogs could be taught to smell the different conditions of their humans, I began to wonder if I wasn't scenting something wrong with Anne. I didn't want Anne to get sick, so I talked with Tabitha."

"You saying I stink?" Anne was biting her lip to keep from crying, and she tried to push Jinx away from her.

Ashur sat down and pushed in tight against Anne's side,

and Jinx melded to her other side. "I'm saying you have an odor as part of your individual scent that is not normal. It's a smell missing from all the other students at your school, and I'm worried it might mean you're sick. Admit it—you're tired all the time, and the smallest bump leaves you with unnaturally colored skin.

"Wait!" Bethany Anne held up her hand. "Meredith, for security purposes, confirm my identity with TOM and ADAM."

It only took a second before Meredith's voice came from the speaker of the security panel at the door where they had all stopped. "Identity confirmed, Bethany Anne."

"Good," Bethany Anne said absently as she entered a code on the pad at the door. She hit the Enter button with a flourish, and the door slid open to reveal a small docking bay with a Kurtherian scout ship in the center. "Everybody in," Bethany Anne ordered, motioning for the others to precede her.

The two dogs and the two other ladies entered the hangar bay and Bethany Anne followed, making sure the door closed and locked behind her. She walked up to TOM's ship and opened the hatch. "Come in," she said as she headed for the room that contained the Pod-doc. "Ashur, you watch the door."

Ashur chuffed in amusement as he laid down in front of the door to the medical room.

Bethany Anne ushered the others inside and closed the door behind her. "Okay," she looked at Anne, "it's just us girls here, so strip."

Anne hugged herself as she looked from Tabitha to Bethany Anne, "Really?" She whispered.

"Jinx is concerned there might be something wrong with you. The easiest and most trustworthy way to run a diagnostic on you is the Pod-doc. For that, you need to be naked." Bethany Anne reached out and pulled the bench from the wall. "You can sit here to take your shoes off. And, yes, really! Myself, Gabrielle and everyone else who has been scanned with the Pod-doc went in naked."

"Well, except for Ashur," a voice came from some speakers in the room. "We didn't need to shave him, so he wore fur."

"True, but not helping, TOM." Bethany Anne sighed in frustration. "We didn't shave the hair off anyone else either, and Ashur doesn't wear ..."

Anne giggled, "It's okay Bethany Anne, I think TOM was just trying to be funny. Hi, TOM, and thanks. You made me feel better," and with that comment, Anne began to undress.

"*Trying* being the operative word relating to TOM," Bethany Anne mumbled under her breath. The remark made Tabitha grin and Anne giggle even more.

**It worked, didn't it? Anne's getting undressed.**

*Don't get such a swelled head that you no longer fit inside mine.* Bethany Anne told her long-time friend, and TOM could hear the smile in her mental voice. *And yes, it worked. You did good, TOM.*

The two women tried not to stare at the array of bruises that were revealed on Anne's arms and legs as she got undressed.

"I'm no doctor, but that's not normal," Tabitha remarked to Bethany Anne as she shook her head.

"You're right," Bethany Anne told her as she entered the

sequence to open the Pod-doc. She looked back at Anne, who stood naked, arms crossed tightly in front of herself, eyes bright with unshed tears as she bit her lower lip.

"I'm scared." The admission was whispered so quietly that without their enhanced hearing neither of the women would have heard her.

Jinx didn't hesitate. She jumped right into the open Pod-doc and laid down tightly against one side of the coffin-like device. "I'll be with you," she reassured Anne.

*TOM?* Bethany Anne asked.

**It's DNA-based,** TOM reminded her, **I don't see why there should be any issue.**

*Thanks,* Bethany Anne said to TOM, then looked at Anne. "It can be difficult coming out of the Pod-doc because you might be disoriented at first, but for the procedure, you just lie down and shut your eyes, then the lid closes and you go to sleep. You won't feel a thing, promise! And I'll be here when you wake up and you will be able to focus on my voice. That will help keep you centered so you won't panic before we get you out of there."

"Okay," Anne replied, trying to be brave but not quite pulling it off convincingly as she climbed into the Pod-doc and laid beside Jinx. Jinx did a belly-crawl to put her head under Anne's hand and licked her wrist. Anne slid her hand under Jinx' muzzle and scratched her chin, then closed her eyes as the Pod-doc's lid silently shut over them.

Bethany Anne had enough time left in her schedule to walk back to Tabitha's apartment. She spent a few minutes discussing current events before needing to go to her next appointment, which just happened to be sparring with Gabrielle and the Bitches. Ashur and Tabitha were long-time friends, so Ashur elected to stay with Tabitha for a while after Bethany Anne left. After sparring came more meetings, then reports that needed to be reviewed. Bethany Anne was reading a report showing the profit the Etheric Empire was reaping from the Pepsi black market when TOM interrupted her.

**Bethany Anne?**

*What's up, TOM?*

**I have the results of Anne's medical scan. After consulting with ADAM, I'm sure that Anne has a form of cancer called leukemia.**

*I've heard the term, but I'm not sure exactly what it is.* Bethany Anne frowned.

**ADAM, you researched it, do you want to explain it to Bethany Anne?** TOM asked.

>> It is a progressive malignant disease in which the bone marrow and other blood-forming organs produce increased numbers of immature and/or abnormal leukocytes. These suppress the production of normal blood cells, leading to anemia and other symptoms. At least, that is the explanation in the medical database I used for reference when TOM asked me to identify the results from the Pod-doc's scan.<<

*How in the nine circles of hell did this happen?* Bethany Anne knew that people younger than Anne could end up with cancer or other dreaded diseases. However, it left her feeling shocked that someone her empire was responsible for could suffer the onset of such a disease without anyone knowing about it. *We can fix this, right, guys?*

**Part of the issue is Sheila Jayden. As you discovered, Mrs. Jayden has not been happy about her family**

joining your empire, so none of the Jaydens have the newest implants. A check of the records showed that the only Jayden to be scanned in the last three years was Mason, and that was job-related. TOM explained the findings to Bethany Anne.

"*Gott Verdammnt*," Bethany Anne spat. "I don't want to go all Big Brother on everyone, but we need to find a way to scan as many people as possible. I'll talk with Cheryl Lynn and Patricia to see if there is some way we can get everyone checked, but that will be for another day. We can fix Anne, right?"

Yes. In some ways, it is similar to what I had to do with you. Re-sequence her DNA and then keep her alive while her bone marrow and other damaged organs regenerate themselves as healthy tissue. However, there may be an issue with being able to limit or control her changes with that invasive of a treatment.

*What do you mean?*

Remember how you had me limit the upgrades some people received?

*Sure. We didn't want to be creating uncontrolled super-people.*

Well, in Anne's case I don't know if I can limit what changes she undergoes and still get her cured.

*Understood. She's a good kid, so please make sure she gets cured. We'll just have to deal with any extras that happen to her as a result, but she's not going to need combat upgrades like reinforced bones and stuff.*

All right. TOM paused for a few seconds before continuing, I estimate her time in the Pod-doc will be five Earth weeks.

*That long?* Bethany Anne was shocked at the timeline.

**Growing healthy bone marrow to replace the infected tissue is not a quick process, and that can't happen until her DNA has been re-sequenced and optimized,** TOM explained.

*ADAM, please email the school informing them of Anne's absence. TOM, go ahead and start the treatment.*

*Tabitha?* Bethany Anne was in go-mode, issuing orders at the speed of thought.

*My Queen?* Tabitha answered.

*Since I didn't address you as 'Ranger,' I don't expect you to give me the 'Queen' bullshit!* It was necessary in a lot of cases, but Bethany Anne really got tired of being called Queen or Empress, *especially* by her friends.

*You rang?* Tabitha's mind voice had a giggle in the background as she tried to imitate the old TV voice.

*Better, and yes,* Bethany Anne answered. *Just letting you know you'll be missing your roommate for at least five weeks. TOM and ADAM say she has leukemia, and it's not a quick fix.*

*But there* is *a fix?* The concern in Tabitha's voice was clearly evident.

*Yes, at least that's what TOM tells me. That's why it's so long in the Pod-doc. Some of the remedies are going to take time to implement fully,* Bethany Anne reassured her friend and Ranger.

*All right, thank you for the update. I was already getting worried that I hadn't heard anything yet,* Tabitha replied.

*I just found out myself,* Bethany Anne informed her.

*Okay, thanks! I'll have Achronyx remind me to check back with you in thirty-three days and see how the treatment is going.*

CHAPTER SEVEN

Bethany Anne tried not to let her concern show as she, Ashur and Tabitha walked into the room housing the Pod-doc on TOM's ship. By ADAM's reckoning, Anne and Jinx had been in the medical device for six weeks, four days, fifteen hours, and twenty-seven minutes. After updating the school since the five-week target period elapsed, Bethany Anne had simply sent a message saying that Anne's return could not be predicted at this time, and she would report for school as soon as she was able.

Tabitha had a terse conversation with Anne's father when he showed up at her apartment one day expecting to visit with his daughter. Mason was yelling that they couldn't keep her away from him when Tabitha finally grabbed him by the shoulders and pushed him against the wall. The fact that the smaller female could manhandle him so easily made a bigger impression than her words.

"Anne has leukemia. Kurtherian science is able to cure it completely, but she's in an induced coma for the treatment," Tabitha was finally able to get through to him.

Mason had just stared at her for minutes before sagging against the wall. After that, the two of them were able sit and discuss the situation.

The last week and a half had been difficult on Tabitha. After the projected five-weeks had passed, Anne's father had begun calling every day. As much as she would have liked to have just told Mason the same thing Bethany Anne had told the school, Tabitha felt sorry for the man. Because of that, Tabitha took all his calls even though all she could say was "still in treatment, I'll have her call you once she's conscious." Now Tabitha stood behind Bethany Anne, trying to look around her Queen's shoulder to see into the Pod-doc.

Anne was asleep one minute and completely awake the next. Before she could panic at finding herself in a coffin-like device, a little window in front of her face opened and she saw Bethany Anne looking in at her.

"There is a latch by your right hip. Feel around with your hand and you'll find it, then just give it a twist," Anne heard Bethany Anne instruct her. It only took Anne a couple seconds to locate and release the latch, and the Pod-doc opened.

"*Cojeme*," Anne heard Tabitha mutter.

"Fut the wuck?" Anne exclaimed as Jinx stood and hopped out of the Pod-doc.

Jinx landed effortlessly and it was easy to see that she was now almost as large as Ashur.

Anne felt as shocked as Bethany Anne looked as she took the proffered hand and climbed out of the Pod-doc herself.

"TOM, you have some explaining to do." Bethany Anne declared to the room.

"Dammit Bethany Anne, I'm a pilot, not a doctor!" TOM's voice sounded from the speakers.

"If you keep trying to misquote Star Trek, you won't even be sleeping on the couch. I'll find a packing crate for your Kurtherian ass and toss it and you into the backyard," Bethany Anne snapped. "What the hell happened?"

"As much as it was a corny take off a TV quote, it happens to be true. I'm not an expert on medicine or the Pod-doc. Because of that fact, a lot of the features are automatic, based on its original programming." TOM sounded somewhat contrite as he tried to explain what he could to Bethany Anne. "I might have been in error when I said that having Jinx in the Pod-doc with Anne wouldn't create any issues. I've never had two beings in the Pod-doc at the same time before."

"So, you just figured—" Bethany Anne stopped mid-sentence as she felt herself starting to vamp out. "All right," she took a deep breath and released it, "what's done is done. First, did the Pod-doc cure Anne's cancer?"

TOM asked Bethany Anne to enter a sequence on the Pod-doc's control panel and studied the readout for several minutes. "Yes, the cancer and all the other genetic issues have been corrected. It's almost like the Pod-doc is learning, the more it gets used. Not only did it repair the DNA for both Anne and Jinx, but it has altered the DNA code to become as efficient as possible."

"What do you mean?" Bethany Anne was confused.

"Remember, my original mission was to create soldiers

to fight on our side. Apparently the Pod-doc's programming has been learning as it's been treating patients. You've been in it, along with Gabrielle and Tabitha. All the Bitches along with Peter and Ecaterina. Ashur and Bellatrix. I'm speculating that treating them has given it more data to work with. While we didn't program in any enhancements, I did not include any sort of restraints on Anne's treatment.

"The same holds true for Jinx. Since it had the data from Ashur and Bellatrix to learn from, Jinx is now the most enhanced canine in the Etheric Empire." As much as he didn't want to be in trouble with Bethany Anne, TOM couldn't help but be a little excited by what the Pod-doc was doing.

>> Is this where I admit that I might be responsible for some of what happened? <<

*ADAM, what do you mean?*

>> I felt your concern and sorrow for Anne's situation. When you said to treat her with no restrictions, I helped the Pod-doc compute the necessary treatments. <<

*How did you do that?* Bethany Anne was confused.

>> The Pod-doc is a Kurtherian device. I'm in a Kurtherian computer. The protocols were already in place. <<

*Well, fuck me sideways! Why did that never occur to me before?*

Could it possibly be because you haven't been able to slow down since you became the Queen Bitch? TOM asked gently.

*You might be right, but I can't afford to miss stuff that*

*obvious and possibly that beneficial to our side*, Bethany Anne said contemplatively.

"What is going on?" Anne's voice expressed her near panic.

"Wait!" Bethany Anne barked. "Something happened, and it's going to take a bit to explain it all. Ashur, Jinx, one of you under each hand. Tabitha, Anne, you two grab an arm and hold tight." With everyone in place, Bethany Anne took a step, and TOM's ship was empty.

---

"I'm still naked," Anne exclaimed.

"Tabitha, get the door," Bethany Anne requested as she grabbed some pants and a shirt from their hangers. "Here. The top will be loose—I seem to be larger up top than you are—but these should work for now." She handed the clothes to Anne. "Come out when you're dressed." And with that, Bethany Anne followed Tabitha and the two dogs into her bedroom.

Anne halted momentarily and took three deep breaths. That drew her attention to the fact that her chest now seemed to be larger. Thankfully it wasn't a ridiculous size, but going to sleep an A-cup and waking up a B-cup meant it would take some time to get used to the change. Anne took a moment to look at herself carefully. Larger bust, check. Wider hips to keep things in proportion, check. Taller...ahh, that would be a "yep" as well. While she hated to get dressed without underwear, she wasn't about to ask Bethany Anne for any, so she pulled up the yoga style pants and tugged the Under Armour tee over her head.

Once dressed, Anne padded barefoot through the door. Bethany Anne and Tabitha were sitting cross-legged on a bed looking at Jinx as she stood beside Ashur. Anne sat on the floor where she could see the other two ladies. Jinx moved over to lie by her side, plopping her head on Anne's thigh.

"TOM," Bethany Anne spoke out loud so everyone could be part of the conversation, "is that Jinx' full size now?"

There was a pause before TOM replied, "From what I can find, most canines aren't fully mature until around two years of age. I believe the Pod-doc optimized her for her current age, so I expect she will still grow some more."

"What about me?" Anne squeaked.

"Have you grown any these past few months?" TOM asked.

"No. I noticed because I was starting to wear clothes out instead of outgrowing them," Anne responded.

"According to the data, human females are normally full grown by age sixteen," TOM claimed. "Since you'd already noticed your growth had stopped, your size should remain what it is currently."

"Thank God for small mercies," Anne muttered. "So, what happened?"

"Well, we found out why you were so tired and were bruising so easily," Bethany Anne started the explanation. "You had leukemia, which you'll be happy to know has been completely cured. As far as your other changes, the Pod-doc optimizes everything. What that means in real terms is that you are now the best possible version of Anne Jayden."

"Wow." Anne looked shocked at the statement. "Is this normal?"

"Think of people like cars for a minute," Bethany Anne explained. "Sometimes they go to the shop just for new tires. Other times it's a tune up. If you were a car, it would be like you went in to check a trouble light. The reason a person goes into the Pod-doc determines what happens to them while they're in there. Your trouble light happened to indicate major work was needed, so we opted for a complete rebuild while you were in the shop.

"That takes more time, right?" Anne asked plaintively.

Bethany Anne nodded. "You're right, it does. You've been in the Pod-doc for almost seven weeks."

Anne's mouth fell open at Bethany Anne's statement. She just sat and stared, unable to voice her shock.

Jinx took the moment of silence to ask, "What about me? Why did I get changed?"

TOM's voice came from the speakers once again. "We're not sure. I hate to keep saying it, but I'm a pilot, not a medical tech. I don't know all the workings of the Pod-doc. I had a mission, to find and enhance combatants for the war against the Seven, so I was trained to make use of the Pod-doc to further that mission. ADAM has speculated that the Pod-doc is learning. The more people who are sent through it, the more it learns what is actually possible for that race's DNA, so it can optimize better.

*Matrix is going to be so jealous.*

Anne started laughing. "You are bad." Her laughter died quickly as Anne noticed the strange looks Bethany Anne and Tabitha were giving her. "What?" she asked the two women.

"Who's bad?" Tabitha asked.

"Jinx. She just said Matrix would be jealous." Anne had a confused expression on her face.

"No, she didn't," Bethany Anne contradicted.

"This isn't funny," Anne exclaimed. "I heard her say 'Matrix is going to be so jealous.'"

*I didn't say it, I just thought it.*

"What?" Anne held up her hand to Bethany Anne and Tabitha as she turned to get a better view of Jinx, who was beside her.

***Are you talking in my head now?*** Anne thought at Jinx.

*It appears so, just like you are talking in mine.*

"Get OUT!" Anne exclaimed as she hugged Jinx. "This is so freakin' cool." Noticing the puzzled looks on the faces of the others, Anne explained, "Jinx and I can talk to each other telepathically!"

"TOM?" Bethany Anne looked toward the ceiling.

"I'm sorry, Bethany Anne, I just don't have answers to your questions." Everyone in the room could hear the frustration in TOM's voice.

"If Anne will permit a link with me, I can research the issue later." A different voice came from the speakers.

"Would that work for you, Anne? Would you mind working with ADAM to find out what happened?" Bethany Anne asked.

"That was ADAM?" Anne enthused. "And no, I don't mind working with him. How do I contact him?"

>> **You were given the latest implant while in the Pod-doc. Not only will it translate all known alien languages for you, but I have just set up a dedicated channel between us.** <<

"ADAM just set up a link in my implant so I can talk to him," Anne told the two women, who had been waiting patiently as they recognized the out-of-focus look in Anne's eyes.

"Lucky bitch," Tabitha grumbled. "You get to talk to ADAM while I have to deal with that reject-of-failed-code Achronyx."

"Considering that Achronyx can travel with you when I need to send my Ranger on a mission, be happy," Bethany Anne chided, then abruptly changed her focus.

"All right, I have a whole bunch of Empress-type work I need to get back to. Anne, you'll need to go shopping again. We'll find some footwear for you. Keep those clothes," Bethany Anne nodded to what Anne was wearing, "and go buy enough to get you through three or four days at least. That way you will have clothes to wear that fit correctly while you shop for whatever else you need. ADAM will set your tablet up to charge your purchases to my account. You'll also need to get used to your new body. The best way I've found to do that is training. Look up Peter in the Guardians' facilities, and he'll arrange an instructor for you. I'll send the school a note explaining your absence, and have them set up a schedule to get you caught up." Bethany Anne took a deep breath as she glanced at Anne, then Tabitha. "Have I missed anything?"

Tabitha and Anne looked at each other, then shrugged and shook their heads. "Can't think of anything at the moment, Boss Lady," Tabitha said to Bethany Anne.

"Good." Bethany Anne smiled at the others. "Anne if you run into difficulties with anything, ask Tabitha for help. If it's urgent and she's not available, use your link with ADAM. He handles most of my administrative tasks anyway, and if he's not sure of something he'll ask." Bethany Anne waved her hands towards her bedroom door and smiled as she told Anne, "Off you go now, I'll check on you later in the week. I imagine it will be an eventful one."

Bethany Anne chuckled to herself as she heard Anne ask, before the door closed behind her, "Isn't that some oriental curse? Living in interesting times."

## CHAPTER EIGHT

Tabitha said she was going to All Guns Blazing, leaving Anne and Jinx to head off to the shopping district. Having been shooed out of Bethany Anne's apartment, still in bare feet, Anne decided the first stop would be for footwear.

"I'm sorry miss, but you can't come in here without shoes." The clerk met Anne two paces inside the door.

"Fine, bring a chair outside then, and you can run back and forth to find what I need," Anne told the clerk.

"That's not possible," the clerk replied in a huff.

"Well, since I don't have any shoes that fit, you need to figure something out," Anne exclaimed with exasperation.

"What, your dog ate all your shoes?" The clerk snarked.

"I. Said. I. Don't. Have. Any. Shoes. That. Fit." Anne bit off each word, becoming angry with the clerk's attitude towards her and the implied insult that Jinx would be so unruly as to chew up her shoes. "Not ... my dog ate all my shoes!"

The clerk took a step back and started to raise a hand as

if to ward off a blow. "I'm sorry, Miss. Please come in and have a seat. Let's start by getting you a pair of socks."

*Well, that got her to change her mind quickly,* Anne sent through her link to Jinx.

Jinx looked up at Anne and replied the same way, *I imagine your eyes glowing red had something to do with it.*

*WHAT?*

Jinx flinched and shook herself. *Not so loud, that hurt!* She couldn't keep the whine out of her voice.

*Sorry,* Anne sent back, *my eyes turned red?*

*Yes, if I didn't know better, I'd say you were related to Bethany Anne.*

*Maybe I am in a way,* Anne speculated, *we're both 'children' of a Kurtherian Pod-doc.*

*I hate to say it, but that sounds creepy,* Jinx replied.

*Kinda, but you're one too.* Anne sent, sticking her tongue out at Jinx.

*That is a thought I really could have done without,* Jinx told the girl beside her.

They had been following the clerk toward the back of the store, and she interrupted their mental conversation. "Just have a seat here, and I'll get your feet measured. Then we'll see if we can find something you like."

Two hours later, wearing a pair of athletic shoes and carrying bags containing five more pairs in different styles, Anne left the store.

*You need more stuff, right?* Jinx asked.

Anne sighed. *Yes, I have to buy another wardrobe in my new size.*

*Why don't you ask for one of those floaty cart-things?* Jinx asked her.

*ADAM?*

>> **Yes, Anne, what can I do for you?** <<

*Oh, cool, it works!* Anne sent happily. She could almost hear the sigh in ADAM's voice.

>> **Of course it works, now what can I do for you?** <<

*Sorry,* Anne replied contritely. *I went from having no implant to being able to talk to the Empire's AI sub-vocally, so it's a big deal to me! What I wanted to ask was, how do I get one of those hover carts?*

>> **Use your tablet and just ask Meredith.** <<

*I don't have my tablet. I went from the Pod-doc to Bethany Anne's to the shopping court for new clothes. I haven't been home yet.*

>> **Ah, female and clothes shopping, now I see the need for the hover cart. Wait one second... There, I have enabled a verbal command channel in your implant. Just say 'Meredith' and it will connect you to the station's EI.** <<

Anne refrained from getting snarky with ADAM over the female-shopping-hover cart comment. After all, she had seen the inside of Bethany Anne's closet. The shoe selection alone indicated that Bethany Anne believed in retail therapy.

*Thank you, ADAM.* "Meredith?" Anne asked quietly.

"Yes, Anne? ADAM just told me you might be calling, what can I do for you?" Meredith's voice came in quite clearly through Anne's new implant.

"I'm going to need one of your hover carts, cuz I have a bunch of new clothes to buy. And, hey, could you get a message to my dad?" Anne asked with sudden urgency, remembering that her dad had probably not been updated on her condition.

"A hover cart is on the way, and yes, I can get a message to your father. What would you like me to tell him?"

"Ask him if he can meet me at the ice cream place in the shopping area." Anne figured that being cured was a good reason to celebrate.

"He says he can be there in twenty minutes," Meredith informed her.

"Thanks, Meredith, that's great!"

Twenty minutes later, Anne and Jinx both stood from where they had been sitting at one of the tables outside the ice cream shop. Anne watched in amusement as her father came to an abrupt halt, his jaw literally dropping when he saw her.

"Baby girl?" Mason managed to choke out. His eyes roamed up and down his daughter's body, trying to make sense of what he was seeing.

Anne took the couple of steps remaining between them and gave her dad a hug. "Hi, Daddy. I've changed a bit."

"I'll say," her father mumbled as he wrapped Anne in a tight hug. "If it wasn't for the dog, and she's changed too, I might not have recognized you."

"Let's grab some ice cream and I'll tell you what's happened." Anne headed into the store, thinking she could really go for a hot fudge banana split right now.

Anne ended up disappointed. There were no bananas in Yollin space, so she had to settle for a hot fudge sundae instead. She, her dad, and Jinx had all finished their bowls of ice cream by the time Anne got to the end of her story.

"And so now I have to shop for new clothes all over again," she said, bringing her father up to the present.

Mason scrubbed his eyes, not wanting his tears to show. "So, you actually *were* sick, not just being difficult," he muttered. "And you're cured now?" he asked, looking for reassurance.

"Yep, I'm all good now," Anne confirmed. "Apparently the Kurtherian Pod-doc-gizmo tweaked my DNA to make sure I'd never be susceptible to that sort of disease again, which resulted in the changes you see now." Anne stuck her tongue out teasingly in an attempt to reassure her dad that she was good with what had happened.

*You're not telling him about the glowing red eyes?* Jinx asked her.

*Nope,* Anne sent back, **between my mom's issues and the changes he can see, he has enough to deal with. There are some things he just doesn't need to know.**

Mason had gotten time off from work to visit his just-out-of-the-hospital daughter, and needed to head back to his job. He gave Anne a hug as they agreed to get together another time soon, and with that Anne's father strode away, whistling a happy tune.

———

Tabitha came home to find Anne on the sofa, Jinx curled tightly beside her while tears ran down her face.

Tabitha rushed over and asked. "What's wrong?"

Anne sniffled a little and used the tissue that had been clenched in her hand to blot her eyes. "I went shopping, and when I got back here I realized I wasn't tired and I didn't hurt." A few fresh tears rolled down her cheeks. "Do you know how long it's been since I haven't been exhausted or in some sort of pain? I got home and unloaded all my new clothes, and it just hit me all at once. I'd spent several hours walking between stores while shopping, walked home carrying in all my bags, and I didn't hurt. I wasn't sore, and I didn't need to lay down for a nap. It's just so overwhelming to think that all that crap is behind me now. Sorry, I don't mean to …"

"Hush!" Tabitha cut her off as she sat on the opposite side from Jinx and wrapped an arm around Anne's shoulder. "I didn't go through what you have recently, but I had my own rough times growing up and I understand what a relief it is to realize you don't have to fight a particular battle anymore."

Anne blotted fresh tears and whispered, "Thanks." Coughing to clear her throat, she continued, "I imagine it will take a few days to accept my new normal."

Tabitha nodded. "Yup, I expect it will, and just when you get used to everything being under control, that *bastardo* Murphy will stick his nose into your business just to prove he can."

"Is that the voice of experience?" Anne asked her roommate.

"That's a big 10-4, *mi amiga*," Tabitha assured her, then stuck her tongue out at Anne's incredulous expression.

"What is this 10-4 and why is it big?" Jinx asked.

Tabitha made a sound that was suspiciously like a snort and looked at Anne. "You know the answer?"

"Sure," Anne replied.

Tabitha patted her on the knee, then stood and headed for the kitchen. "I'll leave it to you to explain then." She heard "Thanks, a lot" quite clearly, but "Citizen's Band and truck drivers" became more of a murmur as she left the room.

---

The next morning Tabitha found Anne and Jinx in the kitchen, already eating breakfast, by the time she got up.

"This is new," Tabitha voiced her thoughts.

Anne kept her head bowed over her plate for a moment, and when she looked up Tabitha could see that her eyes were bright with unshed tears. "I had gotten so used to the pain and fatigue, I didn't realize just how bad it was until it was gone. Besides, since we came out of the Pod-doc it's as if both of us are starving. My empty tummy is what really got me up this morning," Anne confessed.

Tabitha remained quiet as she poured herself some coffee and dropped a couple frozen pastries in the toaster. Once equipped with caffeine and food, she sat by Anne. "Well, make sure you don't stuff yourself. Bethany Anne wants me to introduce you to Peter today to get you some physical training."

Anne didn't look happy about the prospect, but nodded. "She said that would be the fastest way to get comfortable with the changes," she agreed, waving a hand down the front of her body.

"Well, she would know if anyone would. The word is,

she spent more time in the Pod-doc than you did, but came out with similar physical changes. I've seen before and after pictures, and except for her face, you wouldn't think it's the same person," Tabitha confided.

Once the three had finished their breakfast, Tabitha led Anne and Jinx to the Guardians' training room.

# CHAPTER NINE

Tabitha looked around the busy room while Anne and Jinx stopped just inside the door. "Peter!" Tabitha called, seeing the person she was looking for.

Peter Silvers, Wechselbalg and leader of Bethany Anne's Guardians, easily heard his name over the noise of all the people training. He looked toward the door and saw Tabitha waving a hand over her head. "Okay, group, take a break," he told the Guardians he'd been watching train. He walked toward Tabitha, and his expression became confused as he neared the Ranger and saw a young woman and a German Shepherd just behind her. There were only seven dogs on the *Meredith Reynolds*, and Peter didn't know any that were Ashur's size.

"Hey," he asked as he got to Tabitha, "what's up Ranger Tabitha?"

"Lucky for you it's just Tabitha today, no Ranger business," Tabitha retorted.

Peter nodded, acknowledging the difference. Even a Wechselbalg of his capabilities would be in serious trouble if *Ranger Tabitha* and her Tontos were after him. "Okay, then what can I do for you?"

Tabitha turned so she could see both Peter and Anne, and explained their visit. "Peter, meet Anne and Jinx. Anne, Jinx, meet Guardian Peter. Anne and Jinx just came out of the Pod-doc, and they underwent some unexpected changes. Bethany Anne figured that working out with your group would be the fastest way for Anne to get comfortable with her... modifications."

"Nice to meet you," Peter acknowledged, as he fought to keep his expression neutral. He'd had a chance to look the two over while Tabitha was making introductions, and he'd realized that Anne was going to be absolutely gorgeous. He wasn't quite sure how the Pod-doc did it, but the females who came out of that device seemed to always be a step, hell, maybe several steps, above normal women. "Jennifer, Joseph," Peter called into the room.

Two heads turned to find the source of the summons, and a young woman and a very fit middle-aged man headed towards Peter and the visitors.

"Anne, Jinx, meet Jennifer. She's a Were, and she will change and show Jinx effective and proven ways to fight in canine form," Peter introduced the young woman.

Jinx stood, her tail whipping back and forth in a small arc. She was almost quivering with excitement. "Really? I get to train too?"

Peter nodded. "A normal-size German Shepherd is a formidable opponent. With you approaching the size of a shifted Were and having the intellect to understand and learn strategy, there is no reason for you not to train."

"Anne." Peter turned back to the young woman as Jinx

and Jennifer headed off to an unused corner of the room. "This is Joseph. He's one of the Guardian Marines, and he'll be able to evaluate you and get you started on a training program."

Anne looked down at her feet, "Okay," she whispered. "I've been very sick for the last while, and I've never done anything like this before."

Peter broke into a big grin, putting a hand on Joseph's shoulder. "And that's why you have Joseph. Before he was recruited by the Etheric Empire, Joseph was a Drill Sergeant in the Army. It was his job to help shape people who had never done stuff like this before into soldiers. You're in good hands."

Peter listened in as he left the two to work things out between themselves.

Joseph: "You've never done any physical training before?"

Anne: "No, sir."

Joseph: "And that is your first lesson. I work for a living. You can call me Joseph or Sergeant, but don't call me sir. When you say sir, I'll be looking around for the brass. Understood?"

Anne: "Yes, si...gent."

Peter couldn't help smiling to himself as he walked out of range.

---

Joseph was quite pleased after an hour's evaluation of Anne. While she seemed to need a demonstration and basic instruction for the exercises he asked her to do, once she got the form correct she was able to meet and exceed the number of reps required of new soldiers.

With the fitness evaluation done, Joseph started Anne on basic self-defense, and that was where he ran into trouble. Anne easily learned the basic dodges and blocks he showed her, but she would not attack or counterattack with any force whatsoever. When he had dealt with young men, they were normally eager to try to land one on their drill sergeant. Taunting her to quit hitting like a girl didn't have the desired effect either. In fact, it seemed to make Anne even more timid.

Peter had been monitoring the situation with Anne and Joseph for the last few minutes, and he walked over to the two. "Take five, Joseph. Let me have a chat with Anne here."

Joseph nodded his thanks and backed off a few feet from Anne and Peter.

"I don't want to hurt people," Anne confessed, looking down at her feet as she shifted her weight back and forth.

Peter surprised her when he told her, "I fully understand that. Buut…" he dragged the word out, "you aren't just protecting yourself.

"There are exactly seven dogs on this station, and you are partnered with one of them.

"Nathan has already killed one person who saw his daughter Christina in wolf form and attempted violence to try to steal her. What are you going to do if someone goes after Jinx?" He saw the shock hit Anne as the idea that someone might try to steal or harm her dog sank in.

"In fact," he pressured, "what if I were someone who wasn't even interested in a live dog? What if I was a trophy hunter who wanted a dog-skin rug in front of my fireplace?"

*Bingo!* Peter saw Anne tense, then had just enough time to think, *Oh shit, this is going to hurt* before Anne's eyes turned red and her hands appeared to be covered by a silver mist. Peter didn't even see Anne move. She was standing in front of him one second, and the next his chest hurt and he was flying backward. Peter hit the floor and bounced, then rolled to a stop, twelve feet from where he had been standing when Anne hit him. His chest hurt, and he looked down at himself to see a burn mark in his shirt. He glanced up to see Anne advancing on him. *Didn't know I was pulling a tiger's tail,* he thought, and shifted into his Pricolici form.

Jinx looked over from where she was having fun learning from Jennifer to see Peter turn into some sort of monster. She noticed a strange sensation and realized it was some sort of energy flowing through her to Anne. Jinx dipped a figurative paw into that stream and found she could siphon off some of it for her own use. Her muscles suddenly quivered with energy. She knocked Jennifer out of her way and in three quick leaps crossed thirty feet of floor to slide to a stop beside Anne.

Anne didn't slow, even when the man she had just hit turned into a monster from a nightmare. She didn't care who or what he was; she'd already given up her home to stay with Jinx. No one but *no one* was going to threaten to hurt her dog.

"*Enough!*" a commanding voice shouted. The man's loud voice held a tone that affected everyone in the room. It even penetrated Anne's rage, and she stopped.

"Teee heee heeee .... Yoooo sstilll hit llikess a ggirll," Peter told Anne.

"Peter, not helping. Change back *now*!" The man commanded.

Peter closed his eyes, and a second later a man wearing torn clothes with a burn mark fading as it healed stood before Anne and the new man. He took a towel one of the others offered him and wrapped it around his waist. "Well, she does," he reiterated. "I haven't been hit that hard since the last time I sparred with Bethany Anne." He smiled at Anne.

Stephen had dropped into the workout area to watch Jennifer spar. He was always entranced by her power and grace. Seeing Peter in Pricolici form with a young woman and a German Shepherd advancing on him left him feeling uneasy. Luckily, centuries of experience had supplied him with a command presence. His shout had brought everyone in the room to a halt. With Peter back in human form, he looked between the Guardian and the girl. "Would someone please explain what is going on here?" He asked.

Stephen suddenly understood Peter's Pricolici form when the young woman's eyes turned red as she stabbed a finger toward Peter claiming, "He threatened to turn Jinx into a rug!"

Stephen couldn't help but raise an eyebrow as he looked at Peter. "Well?"

"Joseph was working with her, trying to teach her some basic self-defense, but she wouldn't attack him so I goaded her to get her angry enough to take a swing at me. Her hand did this weird glowy thing, and since she hits as hard as a vamp, I figured I needed whatever edge I could get until she calmed down," Peter explained.

Stephen looked around the room and called, "Everyone back to work. Peter, young lady and the young lady's dog, come with me." Stephen led the group out of the workout area and down the corridor to one of the mess halls. "Grab something if you need it, and sit." Once everyone was seated, he looked at the young woman. "I don't think we've met. I'm Stephen."

"Anne, sir, Anne Jayden," Anne squeaked.

Stephen reached over to Anne's clenched hands and laid his hand on hers. "You may not wish to hear this, but you are no longer Anne Jayden. You are Anne. It has been a tradition for a thousand years now that when a person becomes a vampire, they give up their last name."

Anne's eyes grew wide and she had to swallow a couple of times before she could get her voice to work. "I'm a vampire?" Her voice climbed an octave in the space of those three words.

"Bethany Anne put you in the Kurtherian Pod-doc for some reason, correct?" Stephen asked, as kindly as he could.

"Yes, I was sick, and it was all that could heal me," Anne whispered in reply.

"That device modifies human DNA. If enough modification is required, the person who comes out of there is enhanced. Because of a programming glitch with the first enhanced humans, they ended up being called vampires. It has become tradition for vampires to give up their last name," Stephen explained gently.

"I was wrong." Anne murmured, remembering her

letter for help from years ago. She had thought it was neat that Bethany Anne's last name was the same as her own first name.

"Correct," Stephen answered. "Before the Pod-doc, Bethany Anne used to be called Bethany Anne Reynolds. She gave up using Reynolds after she came out."

"That sucks! You mean I have to be just Anne for the rest of my life? Bethany Anne is cool. Anne, not so much," she groused.

Jinx put her head on Anne's leg, offering support. *I don't care what names other people call you, you'll always be my person!*

Anne slipped out of her seat to kneel and hug Jinx. ***Thank you! I really needed to hear that.*** Anne settled back into her seat and gently rubbed Jinx' ears.

"Now we need to discuss your concerns with hurting people," Stephen said, giving her his full attention.

"Bad people hurt others. Bad men had me tied to my bed, rigged to blow up if I tried to move," Anne shot back. "I don't want to be a bad person."

Stephen was confused, and it showed in his expression. He looked at Peter and raised an eyebrow questioningly.

"Trophy wife," Peter mouthed.

Stephen flashed Peter a thumbs-up to indicate that he understood the reference and looked back at Anne. "You know that Bethany Anne killed those men, right?"

Anne's eyes went wide in surprise. "She did?"

"Yes. Over the many years I've been alive, there has been a saying about great power having great responsibility." Stephen kept his voice low and even, trying to ensure that Anne listened to and understood what he was telling her. "Those men had already demonstrated that they were willing to blow up an innocent girl to get what they wanted. If Bethany Anne had let them go, what would have stopped them from blowing up a different girl another time?"

"Ummmm, I dunno," Anne mumbled.

"No one, myself included, wants you to go around beating people up just because you can. A person who does that is a thug and a bully, right?" Stephen turned his statement into a question to keep Anne involved in the conversation.

"Absolutely," Anne replied.

"However, there are a lot of thugs and bullies in this world." Stephen shook his head with a wry smile. "I'm an old man, and still not used to the idea we live in an occupied universe. Since Christina, a nine-year-old girl, has already been threatened with abduction, I think it's fair to say there are thugs and bullies in the *universe*. Now comes the tricky part: should you stand by and let weaker people be hurt just so you don't have to get involved, or use your power to protect them?"

Anne looked both frightened and thoughtful as she sat pondering Stephen's question. Knowing the answer would need to come from within the young lady, Stephen and Peter waited quietly.

*What do you think?* Anne looked down at Jinx.

*My sire fought the bad things. His human fights the bad things. Bad things need to be fought.* To Jinx it was simple: evil things should not be allowed to exist.

"What makes Bethany Anne fight?" Anne asked.

"Justice."

Having been alerted by Meredith about the issue with Anne, Bethany Anne had arrived in the doorway in time to hear the question.

"While the mission has grown with the knowledge of the Kurtherians, I fought for justice way back before I even knew they existed and were a threat. The fact that people had been murdered by others who had gotten away with it just turned my stomach. Even though they were dead and catching their killers wouldn't bring them back, knowing those murderers were behind bars and couldn't kill some other poor soul was what motivated me to get up and give one hundred and ten percent every day." Bethany Anne pulled out a chair, spun it around, and sat with her arms across the back.

"Isn't hurting people bad?" Anne asked.

Peter and Stephen could see Anne was more comfortable talking with Bethany Anne, so they sat back to watch the magic that was the Queen Bitch.

"You forget intent. That's why some courts allow an insanity plea. If the person committing the crime truly didn't understand that what they did was wrong, then they may get special dispensation. Most people, however, know right from wrong, and they chose to do wrong for any number of reasons." Bethany Anne paused to give Anne time to process.

"Like money?" Anne asked her.

"Money, power, love, revenge, just because they get some sick wacko thrill from hurting other people. All sorts of reasons," Bethany Anne agreed. "People don't agree on who came up with it, but years ago someone said 'The only thing necessary for the triumph of evil is that good men stand by and do nothing.' I just can't stand around and let them get away with it.

"There are a couple of other sayings from Earth: 'With great power comes great responsibility,' and 'Absolute power corrupts absolutely.' I found that the more I had to deal with some of the worst of humanity, the more I wanted to just kill them all and let God sort them out. But it would not be a good way to do things, and that's why I created the Rangers. I have them look into situations to decide who's guilty and what punishment fits the crime." Bethany Anne reached out and scratched Jinx' neck. "What's Jinx say?"

"Stephen said that earlier, the thing about great power." Then Anne giggled, despite the seriousness of the conversation. "Jinx says bad things need to be fought."

Bethany Anne nodded. "Well, I think it's true. I know there will be people who ask why my people and I get to be the ones to decide who's bad, but that's something I can live with. I don't choose people with questionable morals. The fact that you are hesitant to hurt other people means I was right when I chose you as one of my people."

"I am? You did?" Anne's eyes were wide with surprise.

"Yes. Ashur and Jinx have an innate sense of good and bad. Since they both liked you, I knew you were a good person inside. Because of that, I didn't try to limit what was done to you while you were in the Pod-doc." Bethany Anne smiled, her tone of voice indicating it was the most reasonable thing in the world.

"Is that why Stephen called me a vampire?" Anne asked.

"You probably received similar treatment to mine," Bethany Anne confirmed.

"So, you want me to fight bad people?" Anne wondered.

"I'm not making you a Ranger or one of my Bitches, and you will need to figure out what you are comfortable doing. I will tell you, so you can think about it, that a lot of people have been injured or killed over the years because someone chose not to get involved when they saw something bad happening. Instead of the bad guys being stopped then, they were able to go and injure or kill someone else. How would you feel if that happened to you?" Bethany Anne didn't want to hurt the girl's feelings, but she knew how she'd react if some slimeball were able to continue to hurt people because she stood by and did nothing.

Anne's face scrunched up with distaste after a few seconds. "Pretty angry." she admitted.

Bethany Anne smiled as she stood. She wrapped an arm around Anne's shoulder and gave her a one-armed hug. "I want you to keep training, and I'm sure you'll figure things out."

Anne stood and squeezed Bethany Anne lightly in return. "Thanks!"

Bethany Anne smiled at Anne, gave Stephen and Peter a finger wave and left the cafeteria.

CHAPTER TEN

Anne had to stop herself from skipping. She'd just gotten the results of her first math test since going back to school.

*One hundred percent!*

She settled for kneeling and hugging Jinx. It was all right for a sixteen-year-old to hug her dog, but not so good to be seen skipping down the hall. She couldn't keep the big smile from her face, however.

She'd been back for four days since she got out of the Pod-doc. Explaining the changes she and Jinx had gone through had been a little challenging, so she kept it simple. "Alien tech was used to cure my cancer, and it had a few side effects." What she found incredible, however, was how easy her school work now was. It seemed that as long as her teachers had good explanations for the material, she could understand and remember everything the first time through.

On a couple occasions when she couldn't understand what the teacher was saying, she had a quick conversation with ADAM. He'd look into the material and show her the proper way to interpret it; turned out the teacher wasn't explaining the subject correctly. That was when Anne found another strange effect from her time in the Pod-doc. *Time.* She and ADAM could hold a whole conversation in her mind in between words of her teacher.

*Anne, this way.* Jinx' mind speech interrupted Anne's musings.

Anne turned and retraced the steps she'd walked beyond where Jinx had turned off.

**What's up?**

*You need to listen carefully, since you still aren't accustomed to using your improved hearing. Mine was always better than humans', so I didn't have to learn to pay attention to it.*

Anne concentrated. **Sounds like fighting. Come on.** Anne broke into a jog, Jinx easily keeping pace beside her.

The corridor that Anne and Jinx were traveling in intersected a hallway that led to another exit from the school. Just past the intersection were four boys, and it took a moment for Anne to figure out what she was seeing. Two boys were holding one while the final one punched him in the stomach.

Anne quickly surveyed the area and noticed this was a hall that did not have any cameras installed yet. Expansion in the commercial sections was happening so quickly that some of the interior areas the aliens didn't have access to were waiting for production to catch up to demand.

"Hey, quit that!" Anne shouted.

The boy doing the punching turned toward Anne and Jinx. "Oh, the freak. You and your mutant mutt can just ..."

**Freak? Mutant?**

*Like I said, you haven't been using your enhanced hearing. They've been calling us that since we got back to school.*

"... stay out of this. We're having a conversation with the faggot here." The boy who was doing the punching snarled at them.

Since everyone had turned to look at her, Anne could identify the boy who was being beaten. Josh Morrison was in one of her classes. He'd been taller than her before the Pod-doc and was possibly just a bit shorter than her current height, so she'd guess he was about five-foot-six. She'd also bet he weighed less than she did now. The fact was, three big strong boys were beating one skinny boy... Wait, the three weren't even *normal* boys. She could pick out their scent now that she was paying attention. They were young Weres.

"It's true," Josh croaked, struggling to catch his breath. "Just go."

Anne looked at Josh, her eyes wide and her mouth hanging open in shock. "So, what?" She finally got out. "You asked them to beat the 'gay' out of you?"

Josh slumped a little in the arms of the boys holding him, trying to get his hands on his stomach. "Oh God, don't make me laugh," he told her.

"What then, did you proposition one of them?" She asked.

"Eww, gross! Not likely." Josh's face was a weird mixture of pain and disgust.

"He was checking us out in the showers," Punching Boy spat.

"You mean, if you were in the girl's shower you wouldn't be checking us out?" She queried.

"What?" Punching Boy looked shocked.

"Oh, naked cheerleaders! That would be totally rad," one of the boys who were holding Josh quipped.

Anne's temper went through the proverbial roof. In a flash of insight so clear it shook her to the core, she understood what Bethany Anne had been trying to tell her. The thought that some people could come across a scene like this and opt to ignore what was going on so they didn't have to become involved made her feel sick. With great power…

"You're just a dirty stinking Were," she snarled at Punching Boy.

"What?" The poor guy was totally confused now.

Anne stepped forward, feigned a punch to his head, then slid sideways to allow herself a full-extension kick to Punching Boy's abdomen. He folded around her foot and flew five feet into the wall and slid to the floor, where he sat dazedly.

"Hey!" One of the boys who had been gripping Josh tried to get hold of Anne. She ducked and spun in one motion, then grabbed his arm and tossed him over her shoulder to land next to Punching Boy.

The boy who'd been pinning Josh's other arm put his hands up and looked at Anne in fear. "What the fuck?"

"Well, since this seems to be Beat-up-people-just-because-they-are-different Day, I figured I'd beat up some stinking Weres," she responded as she took a step toward him.

"I figured I'd beat up some stinking Weres." Christina Bethany Anne Lowell heard those words as she exited one of the doors of the school.

She was only nine years old and not in a position to speak for all of the Weres on the *Meredith Reynolds*. But considering who her parents were, she held some influence, even as young as she was.

She dashed down the corridor and turned the first corner. Due to the age difference, she didn't share any classes with the girl who stood in front of her, but she recognized Anne Jayden and her companion Jinx from having seen them in the halls at school.

Christina saw two Weres who were piled on the ground against the wall. There was a boy whom she could smell was human kneeling on the floor holding his stomach in obvious pain, and another Were was busy backing away from the Jayden girl. Christina shrugged out of her backpack in case she needed to shift. If male Weres were trying to get away from the girl, there was more going on here than she knew.

"What do you have against Weres?" She challenged the older girl.

---

Anne heard a girl's voice ask what she had against Weres. She turned to face the girl, who looked somewhat familiar although Anne couldn't think why. "Nothing, except for maybe when Peter beats on me too much during practice," she said, her nose wrinkled in disgust.

"I heard you say 'beat up some stinking Weres,'" the young girl contradicted.

"Yup," Anne agreed.

The young girl shook her head with confusion. "They can't help being Were."

"I know," Anne told her. "No more than Josh here can help being homosexual. But that didn't stop these mutts from ganging up on a defenseless human."

It took the girl a few seconds to process that information, then she held out her hand to Anne. "Christina Lowell," she offered.

Anne took her hand in her own, "Anne," she replied.

Christina didn't miss the significance of being given only a single name. Her father had told lots of stories about vampires, and according to him the best place to be when a vampire was around was anywhere else. "So, what happened?" Christina asked.

"Apparently Josh here," Anne pointed at the human, still on one knee, "likes boys. Which, if you aren't a raging homophobe," she glared at the two Weres, who were just getting back to their feet, "you would know he has no more control over than you do being Were." Anne turned her head to scowl at each of the three Weres in turn. "Do you think he likes being beaten up because he's ..." Anne used air quotes, "wired differently?"

"But he ..." Punching Boy had finally made it back to his feet.

"Did he hit on you? Try to touch you inappropriately?" Anne asked, while Christina watched.

"He was looking at us in the showers," Punching Boy once again offered as an excuse.

"Oh FFS, if you weren't a first-class slime ball, I might want to check you out. Do you mean to tell me you don't 'check out' pretty girls?" Anne asked in frustration.

"Well, yeah," the boy leered at her.

Anne darted over, grabbed him by the neck, and slammed him against the corridor wall. Punching Boy scrabbled at her arm, his feet kicking futilely as she easily held him off the ground with one hand.

Christina recognized the hypocrisy of Punching Boy's answer. "You want me to hold his arms while you smack him?"

"Thanks, but not necessary," Anne replied, and demonstrated by lightly cuffing Punching Boy with her free hand.

Christina smiled at how easily Anne handled the Were. "FFS?" She wondered out loud.

Anne grimaced. "You know Bethany Anne's rule about cussing?"

It was Christina's turn to make a face. She vividly remembered all the push-ups her parents had made her do when she'd repeated some swear words. "Yup, know it all too well."

Anne couldn't help but smile at Christina's disgust. "For fuck's sake," she whispered. "If I just use the initials, I don't end up with endless push-ups. It's not quite as satisfying as actually swearing, but the tradeoff in push-ups is worth it."

"What's going on here?" A woman asked in a slightly accented voice.

Ecaterina normally waited for Christina to get home from school, to help her with her homework if needed. When Christina was later than normal, Ecaterina had made her way to the school to look for her daughter.

"Hi, Mother. I was just watching Anne *talk* to these boys about bullying in school," Christina replied as she walked back to where she had dropped her backpack.

Ecaterina may not have seen what had preceded the current situation, but she was intelligent enough to figure out who the bullies were when three Weres were involved with one human boy. "Why don't you let him down, young lady, and I'll take them to have a *talk* with my husband."

Anne knew who Ecaterina was, and by default, who her husband was. She couldn't keep the smile off her face as she watched Punching Boy and his friends go pale. "Certainly, ma'am," she acquiesced, opening her hand to let Punching Boy fall to the ground. Anne watched as Ecaterina put an arm around Christina and started her down the corridor saying, "Come along, little wolf," and, sweeping the three Weres with her gaze, she continued, "and you sheep follow as well."

As the five Weres left the area, Anne went over to Josh and offered a hand to help pull him to his feet. "Are you going to be all right?" She asked him.

"I'll be bruised for a few days, but that is nothing new," he informed her.

"You mean this has happened to you before?" Anne was outraged.

Josh wanted to take a step or four away from the girl whose eyes had just turned blood-red. However, considering she had just rescued him, he managed to hold his ground, and reached out to grab her arm when it looked like she was going after the Weres. "If not them, then it would be another group of guys," Josh replied bitterly.

"That's not right!" Anne was in a righteous fervor.

"It is what it is," Josh said, shrugging carefully, mindful of his still sore abdomen, and started to leave.

Anne watched, still very upset about the beatings, as Josh carefully headed down the corridor. "Meredith," she said quietly as she and Jinx continued their journey toward the apartment they were sharing with Tabitha, "let me tell you about some of the things that are happening around the school, things you need to be on the lookout for."

# CHAPTER ELEVEN

It had been a week since the incident with Josh and the Weres, and Anne was finally starting to accept her new self. She had gone from struggling to pass to the top of her class in grades.

Even after daily workouts with the Guardians and Guardian Marines, she still seemed to have more energy than she knew what to do with. While she didn't want to be seen as sticking her nose into Josh's business, her talk with Meredith had resulted in cameras being installed and ensured that Josh was constantly monitored to and from school. She hadn't noticed any new signs of abuse.

Some of the Weres looked at her like she was a skunk or porcupine to their wolf, but since she had never been a popular person in school it didn't bother her at all. She did have to resist the temptation to go all vampire on some of them just to see if they'd put their tails between their legs and run. And despite her tribulations with the Weres and her historical lack of friends, she was slowly being accepted by some of her peers.

Jinx looked up from where she was walking beside Anne. *You are thinking evil thoughts again, I can tell from your expression.*

**Umm, possibly?** Anne tried to make it sound like a question.

Jinx chuffed her version of a laugh. *Admit it, you like that their hackles go up when you get close.*

**They're lucky I don't show them what Josh went through and make them fear walking to and from school.**

*You aren't that sort of person. That's one of the reasons I chose you. You are a protector, not someone who hurts others just because they can.*

**Does it make me a bad person that I can think about it?** Anne was trying very hard not to cry after hearing Jinx' unconditional approval.

Jinx kept pace with Anne as she thought about the question. *I don't think so. There are times during training when I feel like I'd really like to take a big chunk out of Jennifer, but I don't truly want to hurt her. That's just my frustration surfacing. I think it's the same with you and those boys. They were bullies, and they are treating us like we were the ones who did wrong. I think it's normal to have some extreme thoughts in a case like that.*

Anne couldn't help but laugh, **I like how you managed to keep it polite by using the word 'extreme'.**

Anne and Jinx normally decompressed after a day in school by walking through one of the parks that had been built in the *Meredith Reynolds*. Anne liked taking some of the smaller paths through the park. It wasn't that she didn't like people, but for the purpose of decompression, the fewer the better. The two of them had only been on the path for about five minutes when a voice caused them both to stop and look at each other.

"F F S, W T F C I G T R!"

Anne had only told one person about her alphabet swearing, so she and Jinx recognized the voice. They resumed walking, and it wasn't too long before they could hear a *thump-thump* noise along with more letters of the alphabet. As they cleared the end of a flowering hedge, they could see Christina banging her head against a tree.

"What did the poor tree do to upset you?" Anne couldn't keep the undertone of sarcasm out of her voice.

Christina had been so absorbed in her troubles that she hadn't even noticed Anne and Jinx, so hearing the voice caused her to spin and take a defensive stance. Shit, her parents would bar her from operations for a month if they knew she'd been taken this unaware.

Seeing Anne and Jinx both looking at her quizzically, she relaxed slightly. Two girls and an extremely large German Shepherd stood looking at each other. Eventually, Anne raised an eyebrow in question.

"What?" Christina asked, just now realizing that she'd missed Anne's original question.

"You were beating up the tree." Jinx chuffed her laugh. "Anne wondered how it had offended you."

Christina looked at Jinx, then Anne, then the tree, and she put a hand to her face and rubbed her forehead. That's when it clicked that they'd seen her beating her head against the tree.

"It's my parents." Christina let out an exasperated sigh. "It's just not fair! They forbid me from some operations because I can't change." She almost wailed her complaint.

"Wait a sec," Anne cut in quickly. "We've seen you shift, what are you talking about?"

"Oh! Wolf is easy. Heck, if you listen to my dad, he swears I was born puppy instead of human." Christina stuck out her tongue as she said this, letting Anne and Jinx know exactly what her feelings on that situation were. "It's the Were combat form Pricolici they want me to change to. No matter what I try, I just can't get angry enough or upset enough to make the change." Christina wailed her frustration.

"Sorry, what? They want you to change into that big form that Peter transforms into occasionally?" Anne asked, trying to understand the situation.

"Yes! And all the Weres who can do it have to be able to get really angry about something to get the shift to work. Look." The end of Christina's arm morphed from a hand to a paw with two-inch-long claws. "I can do *this*, but I can't change! It's not my fault I haven't experienced anything I can get that mad about," Christina complained.

Anne frowned. "Something just doesn't sound right about that." She held up her hands to placate Christina, who had started to bristle. "I'm not arguing or saying you're wrong, it's just that from the position of someone who's never heard about this before, something doesn't make sense. Come on, let's get you home." She put her words into motion by wrapping an arm around Christina's shoulder and beginning to walk towards the entrance. "I'm going to do some research and see if I can figure something out that will help you."

Christina had been subtly resisting Anne's movement. "Really?" She asked.

Anne nodded and smiled at the younger girl. "Not promising results, but I'll do my best to help you figure this out."

With someone willing to help her, Christina stopped resisting and accompanied Anne and Jinx from the park.

---

The next day Anne hurried from school to the main training room. She and Jinx pushed into the women's locker room and found Christina changing from her school clothes into workout gear.

"Wait!" Anne called to Christina. "Get back into your school clothes."

Christina turned toward Anne with a confused look on her face. "What … why?"

"Pricolici. I thought about your situation last night and I think I might have figured out your problem, but I want us to be alone so we can work on it without an audience. Tabitha won't be home now, so let's go to my place and I'll explain."

Christina looked at Anne and then Jinx. "You're not pulling my chain, as my dad would say?"

"What? No!" Anne felt a little hurt that Christina would even think such a thing. She straddled the bench and sat so she was facing Christina. "I think it has to do with energy. If you channel your anger you can hit harder, right?" Anne waited for Christina to nod in agreement before she continued, "Anger releases adrenalin, which lets your muscles work more efficiently. I think that's what your mom and dad do when they change. They think of something that makes them angry and then they channel the energy those emotions create to change form. That's why not all Wechselbalg can turn Pricolici. Their anger either doesn't create enough energy, or they are unable to channel the energy well enough to achieve the form."

"You think you have a way of getting me angry enough?" Christina asked, still not quite sure she understood the older girl's plan.

"No." Anne smiled as she shook her head. "I want to find an energy source that isn't based on your emotions."

"But that's not how it's done." Christina complained, her confusion was clear in her expression.

Anne held a hand up. "Wait. I'm going to tell you a stupid little story that I heard from my mother."

"When my mother was a little girl, my grandma taught her how to cook. When she was cooking a roast, she always cut the end off the roast. Mother asked Grandma why she did that, and Grandma said it was what her mother had done. My great gran isn't alive anymore, but she was still alive when this happened, so the next time my mother visited her, she asked about the roast. You know what the answer was?"

Christina shook her head, completely baffled by the conversation.

"Apparently my great gran didn't have a pan big enough for the roast to fit into, so she had to trim it to fit the pan. My grandma did have a pan big enough to fit a normal-sized roast, but she cut the end off because that was what her mother had done." Anne started to giggle at the open-mouthed look of shock on Christina's face.

"You're saying we've been cutting the end off the roast?" Christina asked in bafflement.

Anne nodded. "Think about it. The Kurtherians have been on Earth for at least a thousand years. No one knew what was happening, and back then it must have been thought of as a curse or magic or a gift from the gods. Humanity wouldn't have been advanced enough to understand the explanation even if they had been given one. It would have been word of mouth, like 'I was afraid my daughter was going to be hurt, and the next thing I knew I was a monster'. Then it would have been that person telling another, 'He told me he was upset his daughter would be hurt'. Given enough time and with every new person adding their own twist to it, the original story might be lost altogether. Thus we have today's information that making the change is anger-based. You don't need an emotional trigger to change into your wolf form, do you?"

"No, just have to think about becoming the wolf," Christina replied.

"Why would it be different changing to Pricolici then?" Anne asked rhetorically. "I just think it needs more energy to switch into that form. It's like walking and running; it uses the same muscles, but it requires more energy to run for an hour than it does to walk for an hour."

"Well, you'd get farther if you ran for an hour." Christina couldn't help but state the obvious.

"True, but you're still powering the same muscles. You just have to run more energy through them." Anne nodded, a big smile on her face.

"You think you have an answer already, don't you?" Christina felt a shiver of excitement.

"I've got an idea I want to try," Anne nodded again, "but it's not something we are going to want an audience for."

Christina started changing back into her street clothes. "If I had a big sister, I'd trust her word. I'm going to pretend you're my big sister and trust you. Please don't be leading me on."

Anne had to wipe her eye as she moved to hug Christina. "Deal," she said quietly. "You can be my little sister. I can't promise it will work, but I *do* promise I have an idea I think will work. Good enough?"

Christina gave Anne a quick, hard hug in return. "That's fair," she admitted. "Honest failure I can deal with. I just don't want to be someone's joke."

"While I can't promise never to pull a joke on you, I *will* promise that it would never be done at the expense of something this important to you." Anne held up her pinky finger.

Christina had finished dressing by then and wrapped her pinky finger around Anne's. "Fair enough," she said with a smile.

---

Anne was sitting on the couch watching a naked nine-year-old on the floor singing "Who's Afraid of the Big Bad Wolf" when the insistent tone of a tablet's messaging app sounded. Considering the tone in question was a wolf howl, Anne knew it wasn't her tablet. Since Christina was ignoring the noise while continuing to sing, Anne dug through Christina's backpack until she found the tablet.

"Shush!" She implored Christina.

"Christina Lowell's tablet, how may I help you?" Anne had swallowed hard before answering, considering the incoming call was identified as "Mom".

Ecaterina looked out from the tablet, a frown on her face. "Wait, I know you. You're the girl who … Anne, you're Anne. I met you a couple weeks ago."

Anne smiled and nodded, fascinated by Ecaterina's accent. "Yes, ma'am. Christina was late because she was helping me with some Weres who were beating up a human."

"You didn't need much help if I remember correctly, but Christina was rightfully concerned about any issues that could involve Weres looking badly because of improper behavior. Is she there with you?" Ecaterina asked.

Anne worked very hard to keep the grimace from her expression. "Yes, ma'am, she's here. She's indisposed at the moment."

Just then Anne had the tablet yanked from her hands. "Hi, Mumsy, watch this!" Christina yelled into the tablet, which she managed to retain hold of as she shifted, to her newly discovered Pricolici form, and started to howl. "Who'sss afffraidd offf theee bbigg …" Christina couldn't continue her song as she began to laugh.

Anne got the tablet back from Christina and noticed that Ecaterina seemed to be stuck between anger and shocked surprise. "What did you do to her? Is she drunk?" Ecaterina was obviously very concerned as she asked the question.

Anne's shoulders slumped a little at the accusation in Ecaterina's voice. "I was trying to help her, and I don't think she's drunk. High, mayb …"

SR RUSSELL & MICHAEL ANDERLE

*"Don't go anywhere!* I'll be right over." Ecaterina cut off Anne's explanation, and the tablet went blank.

---

Bethany Anne was in the middle of a discussion with Kael-ven about the rebel situation that still existed in parts of Yollin space.

"Bethany Anne." Meredith's voice came from the speakers in the meeting room.

"Hold on, Meredith," Bethany Anne said.

>> **Bethany Anne.** <<

*Wait a minute,* ADAM

**Do you remember the times you told me to wait, only to curse yourself for not listening to me sooner?** TOM asked as quickly as he could.

Bethany Anne sighed silently and switched to vampire speed. *Yes I do, and you're right. What's going on?*

**It appears that young Anne has tried to help Christina with a problem. There have been some unintentional consequences, and Ecaterina is now on her way to Tabitha's place. She seems to be in Were-mother-needing-to-rescue-her-offspring-mode, and I don't know if she'll be willing or able to listen to reason.**

*If I'd known how badly this job sucked, I don't think I would have taken it on,* Bethany Anne griped to TOM.

**Yes, you would,** TOM told her. **Your sense of right and wrong would have made you do it anyway.**

Bethany Anne sighed as she dropped out of vamp speed. She looked across the table to see Kael-ven holding up a hand.

"Get back to me when you can," he told her.

"What?" Bethany Anne raised an eyebrow in surprise.

"You get a certain expression when you're talking with your lodgers," Kael-ven explained. "I imagine it's something serious for them to interrupt you, so go deal with it and get back with me when you can."

Bethany Anne rose from her chair. "Sorry ..."

Kael-ven just waved her off. "I truly do not know how you function, with everything that you have to deal with."

Bethany Anne chuckled. "I function by cutting short meetings with my head of government," she said, then took a step and vanished.

Kael-ven hadn't really been happy about having his meeting cut short. However, the manner in which Bethany Anne departed confirmed that something important had come up.

---

Ecaterina couldn't get to Tabitha's place as quickly as she wanted to. She was upset at that Anne girl and so afraid for Christina that she feared she'd shift unintentionally if she didn't keep her feelings and actions under tight control. What she *didn't* expect was to see Bethany Anne leaning casually against the front door of Tabitha's apartment.

"What are you doing here?" Ecaterina came to a stop in front of Bethany Anne.

"Got a bat signal," Bethany Anne answered, pointing to her temple. "Said you were about to go off half-cocked."

Ecaterina slid to a stop. "What is this 'half-cocked'? I haven't heard that before."

"It's from early firearm days when you had to pull the hammer back with your thumb. There was half-cocked, which was supposed to be safe, and full-cocked, which was ready to shoot. Look it up when we're finished here if you want a better explanation. Let's find out what's going on." Bethany Anne tilted her head in the direction of the door, only to freeze when the door opened behind her.

Anne looked pale as she moved away from the door; having any angry Were-mother headed toward you would do that to a person. "Hurry, she doesn't know I've left yet." Anne turned and went back into the living room.

Bethany Anne and Ecaterina followed Anne and found Christina curled up on the end of the couch, fast asleep in wolf form. Jinx was curled beside her, watching the people as they entered the room. Bethany Anne grabbed Ecaterina's arm before she could rush over to her daughter. "She doesn't look to be in any danger, so let's hear what happened before we do anything." she cautioned, keeping her voice steady in an attempt to keep the situation calm.

Ecaterina pulled her arm from Bethany Anne's grip but nodded her head sharply once to indicate that she would stay calm, for now.

"What did you do to her?" She whispered angrily to Anne.

"End off a roast." Everyone turned to see Christina sitting beside Jinx in human form.

"Oh, my head hurts," she whined, bringing her hands up to cover her eyes.

Bethany Anne went into the dining area, grabbed two chairs, and set them opposite the couch. She looked at Ecaterina and pointed to one chair as she sat down on the other. "End off a roast?" she asked, looking at Anne, confusion evident on her face.

Anne looked at the still-scowling Ecaterina and decided this was not the time for cute stories. "Christina was unhappy that she couldn't shift into the Were combat form. I had an idea I thought would help her, and told her a story to explain why I thought my idea might work. It had to do with cutting the end off a roast."

"What was your idea?" Bethany Anne asked, looking at Ecaterina with a 'let me handle this' expression.

"Well, she told me about not being able to shift, but it didn't quite make sense to me, the way she said Weres shift to that form. And since she can morph her human arm into a Were paw with big claws I knew it wasn't lack of control, so I thought she simply needed to be able to tap more energy." Anne saw that Ecaterina was losing patience with her explanation. "I gave her a vial of my blood to drink," she finished in a rush.

Ecaterina looked shocked while Bethany Anne looked frustrated. "That makes a certain sense, it's how we vamps tap energy from the Etheric. No one warned you that vamp blood and Were blood don't mix well, did they?"

"NO! It was never mentioned. I swear I never thought it would harm her. Is that why she's drunk or high or whatever it is that's happened." Anne looked steadily at Ecaterina as she said this, hoping that the woman would see the truth in her statement.

Bethany Anne got the far-off look that meant she was talking to her internal companions. "TOM says that's probably a side effect and he says if Christina was older her reaction would probably have been more severe. Did she drink it all?" Bethany Anne asked.

"Eeww, that's not good." Christina moaned as her head moved when she went to nod in response to Bethany Anne's question. "It tasted disgusting, too."

Ecaterina's expression was a mix of worry and pride. "Will she be alright?"

"Fu …" Bethany Anne cut off one of her famous curses when she saw Ecaterina lift a hand to swat her. "Sorry," she muttered to Ecaterina. "Can you still shift now?" she asked Christina.

Christina peeked through the fingers of one of the hands that still covered her eyes. When she saw that Bethany Anne was serious, she mumbled, "Dunno." A frown of concentration, and then there was a five-foot-tall Pricolici in the spot that a four-foot-tall girl had just occupied.

Anne turned as the motion from the end of the couch caught her eye.

"Telll meee I wasnnn't ssingingg bigg badd wolfff." Christina looked at Anne hopefully.

Everyone in the room was surprised when Ecaterina burst out laughing. "It's going to be awhile before I let you live that down, little wolf," she teased her daughter. "I even have a copy of it on my tablet."

"Someone just shoot me now," Christina grumped after she shifted back to human form, but then she screeched in embarrassment as it finally dawned on her she was sitting there naked. Arms now protectively crossed over her chest, she looked at Anne, who pointed to an end table that had a pile of neatly folded clothes sitting on top of it. Christina grabbed them and started dressing.

Bethany Anne's suddenly tense posture brought all eyes to her. "TOM is pretty sure there will be no lasting damage, but bring Christina to the Pod-doc if she exhibits and unusual symptoms. You can tell Nathan," Bethany Anne said, looking at Ecaterina, "but other than him, this information goes no further!" She waited until everyone including Jinx nodded their acceptance of her decree.

Bethany Anne looked at Ecaterina. "You good now?"

Ecaterina nodded to Bethany Anne, then walked over to Anne and pulled her into a hug. "I'm sorry for how I acted," she told the young woman. "Most mothers are protective of their children, but I think Weres carry it to extremes."

"It's okay. I really didn't know there was an issue, nor that it would affect her that way," Anne offered contritely. "I would not have suggested it if I'd known."

Bethany Anne stood and placed a hand on Ecaterina's shoulder. "Why don't you take Christina home and put her to bed? Let me know if there are any complications."

Ecaterina nodded and wrapped an arm around Christina, then mother and daughter left.

"Sit!" Bethany Anne commanded, her finger pointing back to the couch. "Explain the 'end off a roast' comment."

Bethany Anne's gaze was so focused that Anne stumbled a couple of times from nervousness as she told her the story.

"You think there is a lot of fiction and misinformation about some of the abilities enabled by Kurtherian tech?" Bethany Anne asked her when Anne had finished.

Anne took a deep breath, then held it before letting it out and taking another. She sat up straight and looked at Bethany Anne. "I don't know if some of it might be intentional, but I am leaning more toward it happening so long ago that there was no understanding of what it was or how it had happened. What's that saying about sufficiently advanced tech being indistinguishable from magic?"

Bethany Anne looked confused, then ADAM spoke to both of them.

**>> Attributed to Earth author Arthur C. Clarke. 'Any sufficiently advanced technology is indistinguishable from magic.'<<**

Bethany Anne regarded Anne, a speculative look in her eyes. "You think we were too barbaric to understand what was happening?"

**I never got a chance to explain anything to Michael, to even know if he was capable of understanding. We didn't even know the wolf-model Weres were Kurtherian until we got one in the Pod-doc. The Weres in China might have known, but that knowledge would have been held secret within the clan.**

Unaware of TOM's conversation with Bethany Anne, Anne tried her best to answer. "I wouldn't have said barbaric, but look how much stuff that we understand today was attributed to gods or demons or witches in mankind's early years. The sun and moon were gods flying across the sky. An eclipse was a dragon trying to eat the moon. Without having a way to prove or disprove an idea anything that sounded half-assed possible could gain traction. 'Oh, our explorers never made it back, well that's because the world is flat and they sailed so far they fell off the edge.'" Anne's snort was very unladylike as she brought her mini-tirade to an abrupt halt.

Bethany Anne's "You have a point" was matched by TOM's **She has a good point.**

"Okay, I, as in Empress Bethany Anne, am going to appoint you as my Etheric Researcher. We'll get ADAM to set up a connection... Oh, he says you already have one. Good, use that to talk with ADAM and TOM and see if you can figure out any more ways we've missed optimal usage of a talent. Hell, see if you can figure out new ways to use what we know.

I'll have ADAM notify Team BMW, Jean Dukes, and anyone else who might be able to help you that you are authorized for assistance and information at the highest levels. Only work that's directly for me or that directly affects our military strength and efficiency will take precedence over your inquiries. The Empire, which is me," she motioned to her chest with her thumb, "will pay you as a junior researcher. That will be reviewable the first time you bring me something that works and has a useful purpose. Bring me an Etheric-powered toilet paper roller and I'll toss you out. Bring me something like a pocket universe shoe closet and I'll give you a duchy somewhere. We clear?"

Anne was having trouble breathing as the magnitude of what Bethany Anne had just proposed sank in. "Crystal," she replied with a grin.

Bethany Anne was headed for the door when she paused and looked back at the young woman, who was frozen in shock. "This is not permission or an excuse to skip school or have your grades fall! ADAM will be monitoring those sorts of things for me." She smiled to take a little of the edge off her warning, and headed back to the duties of an Empress.

Anne waited for the door to close, then jumped up and down before dropping to hug Jinx. "I've got a job!" She shouted. "I'll be able to pay people back and buy stuff for us both without having to feel guilty about sponging off others."

"Does that mean I'll get steak more often?" Jinx asked hopefully.

"I won't know how often until I find out how much a junior researcher makes, but we can celebrate with steak tonight for both of us!" Anne spun and headed for the bedroom to change into clothing appropriate for dining out.

*Just wait till I tell my dad*, she thought with a smile.

# CHAPTER TWELVE

Tabitha opened the door to her suite and called for her roommate as she strode in. "Anne?"

She walked over to the kitchen table and dropped off her tablet. Turning around, she noticed Anne and Jinx coming out of her room.

"Hey, R2, what's up?" Anne quipped.

Tabitha shook her head. Now that she was on the receiving end of playful nicknames, as she would commonly do with Barnabas, it could be quite annoying from those much younger than oneself. Saint Payback truly *was* a bitch.

"It's not R2, it's not Ranger Two, it's not Queen's Ranger Two, it's not just '2,' the name is Tabitha. It's also not Tabby, with a 'y' or Tabbi with an 'i.'"

She eyed the young woman.

"How about Tabbie with an, 'ie'?" Anne smiled, wondering what the Ranger would say next.

"If a few of the Tontos and I didn't need to leave shortly, I would make you eat those questions. Further, I don't think you have enough bruises on your body for the amount of workout time that you've been spending." Tabitha raised an eyebrow as she looked the teenager up and down.

Anne quickly shook her head. "Nope, workout time won't be necessary. Tabitha is what you want to be called? Tabitha is what you will get. As for the bruises," she waved a hand up and down her body "Bethany Anne suggested that as a researcher, I needed to know self-defense, but did not have to work out as hard as all of the rest."

Tabitha drew her eyebrows together. "Is that the truth?"

Anne looked at her roommate and bit her lip, finally deciding to nod her head in the affirmative.

*Bethany Anne?*

*What is it number two?*

Tabitha rolled her eyes before responding, *is it true that you told Anne she didn't need to work so hard on her physical training because she was going to be doing research?*

*No, have you ever known me to suggest such a thing?*

*No, I haven't. So, you can imagine my surprise when your new Etheric Researcher suggested that this was exactly what you had said.*

*Huh, so my new Etheric Researcher is acting all teenagerish, am I understanding you correctly?*

*That's the way it appears.*

*Okay, since you have to go out with the Tontos on the slave issue, I'll make sure to take care of this with Peter. He should have some insights on recalcitrant teenagers and getting the best results out of them.*

*Very well, I will consider this a closed issue.*

Bethany Anne added, *You can let her know that Peter is*

*going to have new instructions, from me, when she is due for her training session three hours from now.*

*Will do, My Queen. Have a great one.*

*You, too. Go kick some pirate ass.*

Tabitha smiled. *Oh, I intend to, this ought to be a hoot.*

*Make sure you say hello to the Twins for me.*

*Tweedledee and Tweedledum? I'll let them know.*

Bethany Anne cut the connection between the two of them. Tabitha raised an eyebrow. "Bethany Anne says that Peter will have new instructions for your workout when you see him in three hours."

"Three hours!" Anne's face opened up in shock. "I'm supposed to be meeting a couple of friends over in the library in three hours."

"I suggest...next time that you do the workouts that you were told to do, instead of trying to get out of them. I especially suggest ..." Tabitha reached up and tapped the side of her head " ... not lying to one of the Queen's Rangers who can talk to Bethany Anne directly."

Anne's eyes closed when she realized her mistake, she turned around and then kicked the air in the direction of the couch. "God, it was so much easier getting away with stuff when it was only my mom and dad."

Tabitha pursed her lips, "I understand you're doing well with your dad now, is that right?"

Anne turned back around to face her roommate. "Yes," Anne shrugged. "I'm okay with it all now, but it was pretty scary in the beginning when I thought I'd be on the outs with my parents."

Tabitha walked over to the young woman and put an arm around her shoulder and pulled her in for a hug. "You don't need to worry about that. Your parents will forgive you, no matter what the problems are. You might just have to give it some time before it happens. They love you, but your mom was under some incredible strain, and she broke. That's nothing against her, and really, it helped a whole lot. Now, we understand classes needed to be created for those of us who aren't coping as well as we had hoped, once we left Earth. Some of us get so involved with the next goal, we forget that a lot of those who are supporting us right now are maybe having their own troubles and difficulties."

Anne mumbled a response into Tabitha's chest, "Brgrlfllrrrckraghen."

Tabitha pulled away and looked down at the teenager. "What did you say?"

Anne smiled. "I said, 'I can't breathe!'" Anne pulled Tabitha back in for a hug before releasing her. "I know that now, but it was pretty scary when the Queen emancipated me in the first place. I'm super excited to be working on the Etheric research, and it's kind of cool that I sometimes get to talk to my dad about it as well."

Tabitha turned and started walking to her own room in the suite. "Well, he did all of that work with that stupid black-ops shell company, so some of this is not that far out from what he was working on."

Her voice came from inside her room. "Who knows, maybe you and your father will become famous for research on Etheric travel!"

Tabitha didn't see the small tear that Anne reached up and wiped away. She waited a moment to get her emotions in order. "Maybe. That would be pretty rad."

Tabitha's voice called back out from her room, "Hey, so, while I go on this operation with a few of the Tontos, what you going to be doing?"

Anne walked to Tabitha's door and leaned against the opening. "I've been told that I will get my own small suite in about three or four days. So, when you get back you won't have a roomie anymore."

Tabitha looked up from the little gym bag of extra supplies she was taking with her. "Really?" Tabitha looked around her room. "God, it will be so good not to have to be so clean all of the time."

Anne looked at her, annoyance on her face. "What? Are you saying you're not naturally this clean?" She pointed around the room to all of the areas that were spotless.

Tabitha chuckled. "Hell no. I'm only this clean because I had a teenager here sharing my suite all of the time. I had to set a good example. If you weren't here, I would have been messy. When I know somebody is coming over, I will throw it all into a basket and stick it somewhere in the back of the closet. I'm not that much older than you for Pete's sake."

Anne continued looking at her roomie, mouth open. Finally, she threw up her hands and turned around. "I'll bet you I'm cleaner than you are without you putting in the extra effort." Tabitha smiled as the young woman walked away.

Two and a half hours later—no way Anne was going to add being late on top of everything else—Anne and Jinx walked into the workout area. When she saw Peter glance over at the clock on the wall and smile, she figured she'd been right to be early. To her surprise, Peter motioned for them to follow him. Anne, with Jinx holding tightly to her side, followed Peter through a door into what turned out to be some kind of office. Peter sat behind the old primer-gray metal desk and motioned to a bench that could double as a seat for some of the four-legged Yollins.

Peter watched as Jinx hopped up on the bench, and had to work to keep the smile off his face as Anne sat nervously beside her dog. "I know that you have been through some issues that could bother anyone. Combat is almost second nature to us Weres, but I can understand why a person might not desire to fight. However, you two have targets painted on you." Peter was amused at the fish-out-of-water expression on Anne's face, and he held up a hand to forestall comments before she was able to get her voice working. "You," he pointed at Jinx, "are one of only seven dogs on this station, and sooner or later some rich person is going to offer enough money that someone is going to try to dog-nap you." He held up both hands while shaking his head to keep the two silent. "Now, if someone puts a bounty on a dog, do you think the slimes trying to poach a canine will go after Bethany Anne?"

Anne and Jinx looked at each other, eyes widening as they went through the list of people who were dog companions.

Matrix and TOM, which also meant Bethany Anne.

Devi was with the two Academy administrators.

Snow was with Kael-ven.

Which left her and Jinx, or… Oh my God!

"Dio is unprotected a lot of the time," Jinx growled.

Peter nodded, smiling like a sensei whose student finally understands. "He's the most vulnerable, so we'll have extra observation on him. But he can hole up with Yelena and Bellatrix and not be seen. You two, however, have school, training, and now work. And that brings us to Point Number Two. Anne, why were you on a bed full of explosives?"

It was clear that Jinx actually connected the dots faster than Anne because she started to growl, hackles up, before Anne replied. "Some bad guys wanted ..."

"The research information that your dad was involved in." Peter finished for her, once again nodding his head. "There are only a couple of us in the know right now, but it's not going to stay secret forever. Once you start working with others, and especially once the Etheric Empire exhibits or implements the results, people are going to start taking a lot of interest in finding out who is responsible for those 'results.'" Peter finished with air quotes on the last word. "If they can link that research back to you, then you, or maybe your parents, are targets. As distasteful as it may be, you're going to have to become another Bethany Anne. Someone who is so powerful and frightening that people will think twice or three times before trying to attack you or those you are protecting."

Peter actually looked apologetic at this last statement, and that more than anything eased Anne's mind some. She still didn't like the idea of hurting people, and she really detested getting sweaty and bruised, but...

*We're going to have to commit and do this.* Jinx sent to her partner, and heard Anne's mental sigh.

*I know, I really do hate bruises though.*

*You bruise less since we came out of the Pod-doc,* Jinx observed.

*You're right, and there's a way to bruise even less.*

Anne looked at Peter and stood. "I believe we have three hours of training scheduled."

Anne turned and led Jinx back into the gym, sending a final thought.

*We need to be the ones handing out the bruises.*

*FINIS*

First and foremost a big THANK YOU to all of you who have read this far.

As a volume reader myself there have been a lot of books that I've started that I was not able to finish, so if this has held your interest long enough for you to get here ... Woohoo!

I've always had a very active imagination, and I've thought of hundreds of stories over the years but I've never tried to publish anything because I've always felt my writing style was too minimalist. Then almost two years ago I had a 'recommendation' from Amazon for a story by some guy called Michael Anderle, and hey, he already had three other books written. So, instead of jumping in at *Bite This*, I happily started *Death Becomes Her*.

A day and a half later and the fateful passage asking for beta readers. Having just recently been placed on long term disability I thought, why not? Now I have the time to do something like this.

I've never claimed to be a professional editor, and I

didn't make that claim to Michael either. However, it seemed I was better than the system he was using at that time and that earned me a seat on the crazy ride of Michael Anderle trying to publish a book a month.

What has this to do with my writing, you ask? Simple … Michael is another minimalist author. He's been living proof if you write a compelling story with characters the readers become invested in, you don't need paragraphs of descriptive content.

One of the things I've done over my years is breeding, training and showing dogs, so when Ashur entered the story I was quite happy. Well except for the messages to Michael complaining that some of the things he was writing were not factual. Probably not a big surprise to him considering all the complaints I had about his firearm information.

Once we had Bellatrix and then puppies, I decided I would try to write a story for one of the pups, and since Anne was already somewhat special in her ability to understand Ashur, it seemed like an obvious match, so I asked Michael to 'save' Jinx for me to write about and you have just read the result. Unfortunately, I type extremely slowly and I can't keep pace with Michael's output. However, now that I've managed to churn out one story I'm working on plot lines to see what sort of mischief Anne and Jinx can get into in the future.

Stay tuned …

# AUTHOR NOTES - MICHAEL ANDERLE

WRITTEN 09/13/17

First, thank you for not only reading through this book, but through STEPHEN'S author notes, *and now mine,* as well!

This book represents (to me) an incredible journey of people helping people, and how each of us can help make dreams come true.

When I was first publishing, just 90 days into my effort to make a living writing (Jan/Feb 2016) I had asked 'for a little help' and Stephen Russell raised his hand and said 'I'll help.'

I can imagine he has wondered about doing that at least once or twice since then.

(Stephen, if you have wondered three times, don't tell me that. Let me live in my little cocoon of ignorance and bliss, please.)

Stephen, like me, read thousands of books...But, he read thousands more than I. As a long haul truck driver, he had beat the shit out of his body over the decades and was willing to do what he could to help another fellow follow some dreams.

Thus was born the Production Editor role. I'll allow Stephen to share more of his story in future author notes (the ****** will author note block me, for sure!)

Stephen was instrumental in becoming the liaison between the Beta Reader teams, and me as I pounded away at the keyboard, threw the (mostly) finished manuscript to him to edit the stupid out and manage the beta reader process.

We still use that core process today with The Kurtherian Gambit series.

Like me, Stephen had a desire to write a book but had never really been able to manage it. We played with a couple of his ideas, and then I talked about how you, the fans, wanted more dog stories. The problem is I'm not really a dog person and don't know dogs extensively, and Stephen does.

How do you think I got German Shepherds into the mix? He was an advocate and had my ear... Or, I just don't remember what I said, and he tweaked the document, and I looked at it thinking "I'm a damned genius!"

(That part isn't true. We did go German Shepherd after a discussion, and he didn't change it after the fact. But that would be funny as hell if he had.)

So, I get to introduce you to my friend, production editor, badass firearm knowledge support and previously a Dog breeder who knows how to help me put out stories.

That includes our furry friends.

WELCOME Stephen Russell to the MADNESS that is authoring in The Kurtherian Gambit.

It is now my turn to laugh my ass off when the fans give you shit!

Ad Aeternitatem,

Michael

OTHER BOOKS BY SR RUSSELL

# WANT MORE KURTHERIAN GAMBIT?

Website:
http://www.lmbpn.com

Email List:
http://lmbpn.com/email/

Facebook Here:
www.facebook.com/TheKurtherianGambitBooks/

www.ingramcontent.com/pod-product-compliance
Lightning Source LLC
Chambersburg PA
CBHW050147110726
47898CB00008B/2706

* 9 7 8 1 6 4 9 7 1 1 6 7 0 *